DAY OF THE DEAD

A GRAY WITCH NOVEL

R.R. BORN

Cover Design by OliviaProDesigns

Cover Photos from Depositphotos/Prometeus/Flotsum

Paperback 978-1-7324337-4-8

Ebook 978-1-7324337-3-1

First Edition - October 2019

Created with Vellum

For all those we lost too soon.

Stan Adams, who always asked,
"You done with that book yet, gal?"
"Yeah, Stan. I'm done."

And
Cindy Chao
You were loved.
Ānxí
安息

DAY OF THE DEAD

CHAPTER 1

Beep, beep, beep.

The blaring alarm wouldn't stop. Ari covered her head with her pillow.

I just laid down, she thought. It couldn't be time for work. Then she smelled it. That wasn't her alarm to get up. It was the smoke detector. The batteries should be dead in that thing, it's gone off so many times this month.

"Cher, you might want to get in there," Remy said.

She moved the pillow just enough to uncover her eyes and still block out the stench. Her ghostly best-friend hovered above her with his hands over his ears. When the second alarm went off, he shook his head and disappeared.

Ari threw back the covers and noticed the little puffs of smoke invading her room from under the door. She opened the door to a wall of thick gray smoke. Waving with one hand and covering her mouth with the other, she made her way to the hallway detector and turned it off.

She thought bringing a person back from the dead would be the most difficult thing she'd do in this lifetime. Wrong! Apparently, it would be teaching a 400-year-old witch how to use the microwave. Why wasn't there a handbook for the recently deceased and resurrected?

Ari fanned the smoke as she walked towards the kitchen. Nyah sat on the sofa rocking back and forth with her ears covered. After Ari turned off the kitchen detector, she called out. "What did you try to cook?"

Remy chimed in, "The Orville."

Ahhhh, popcorn. The smell of hot, buttery popped corn could be the best aroma ever or when burnt like now, be the absolute worst smell imaginable. She flipped the bag into the sink and doused it with water to put out any lingering odor and clear some of the smoke.

Once the stove's overhead vent whirled to life, the smoke moved, but not fast enough. "Nyah, could you open the patio doors, please?" She fanned with a long, thin magnetic notepad from the fridge.

Remy leaned over to look into the living room. "Try it again, Cher."

"What? Why?" She mimicked him and followed his gaze. Nyah had stopped rocking but hadn't moved from the couch.

"Good goddess," Ari mumbled before walking back into the room. She sat next to Nyah and touched her back, the young woman stilled. "Nyah, it's okay. It was only popcorn."

"You might want to get her out of the building before she burns the place down," Remy said.

Ari cut her eyes at him but held her tongue. For whatever reason, since the day Nyah walked into her place he hadn't liked her. She knew Nyah wouldn't stay here forever, but this was the only solution for now.

"Nyah. Look at me." Red-rimmed eyes slowly turned towards her. "This is a lot to get used to. Don't get bent out of shape about it."

Nyah's eyes widened. "What?" She looked at her arms, then touched her body. "I'm going to bend?"

"Oh, no." Ari grasped the young lady's now flailing arms. "That's just a saying." *Oh, boy.* She reached for both of Nyah's hands. The girl might have a heart attack at this rate. Ari was so awful at the whole consoling thing. She needed to get this girl to her man, pronto.

"Breathe." Ari overly exaggerated the breathing process with pouty lips, to get Nyah to follow her lead. After two minutes, or so, they were both inhaling and exhaling in regular intervals and Nyah looked a lot calmer.

"Okay. You want something to drink?"

Nyah nodded and Ari released her hands.

Ari opened the patio sliding doors first, then to the kitchen. She held the kettle under running water to brew a pot of chamomile tea. Then considered the state Nyah was in and changed her mind.

"Time to pull out the big guns." Remy waved towards her small wine rack.

"Yeah, I think you're right." Ari pulled two goblets from the shelf and dusted off a bottle of merlot. She wasn't a big wine drinker but kept both on hand for those who did. And she wasn't averse to a good Riesling now and again. She opened it and let it breathe.

"Cher, when is she leaving?" Remy stood with his arms folded.

Although Nyah couldn't see or hear him, she would hear Ari's response. She lowered her voice as much as she could. "Remy, what do you have against her?"

It's a weird thing to see a ghost tighten his lips and roll his eyes. But Remy had perfected the look over the years. "I get a bad feeling when I'm around her. I just don't trust her."

"Well, I'm working on it. It won't be too much longer."

She poured two glasses of wine. One a little fuller than the other, as she didn't need anything to help her sleep. Nyah, on the other hand, couldn't hold her liquor. Rookie.

After making Nyah take three good gulps of wine, she seemed to loosen up. She sat crossed-legged on the couch, then leaned over to grab a stack of papers from the side table.

"Aria, I went down to the metal box." Nyah's accented English sounded more like the Queen's English.

For whatever reason, Nyah hadn't been able to say her name correctly. A breathy 'A' happened at the end every time. Finally, Ari stopped trying to correct her and just let it go. No one else called her that and it sounded nice in Nyah's weird accent.

Ari took the mail. "Did…?"

Before she could finish, Nyah shook her head. "No one saw me. I covered my hair and put on these." She lifted a pair of mirrored shades from the coffee table. "I did good, yes?"

Ari held her glass out. "Yes, you did well." Nyah clinked her goblet to Ari's in a toast. They had agreed to two things, one Nyah needed to protect her identity. And she needed to wear clothes. Nyah was absolutely okay with her nudity.

They watched a movie with some properly popped popcorn with extra butter, but Nyah nodded off after the second glass of wine. Ari flipped through channels and stopped on the news for the weather. She muted it when a report about the hospital came on and thumbed through her mail while she waited. It was mostly bills, but the one thing she'd been waiting for had finally appeared.

A postcard.

One side had a glossy picture of an old, red brick Dublin pub, complete with an antique-styled sign that read: "Guinness, sold here by the pint." She flipped it over, her bestie's boxy, square letters filled the back. Her friend had tried to call a few times but with spotty service and the time difference, they kept missing each other.

Leise and her new boyfriend, Brennan were traveling through and around Ireland to help him find and possibly reconnect with his family. Brennan's quest was damn near impossible and difficult at best because his uncle had locked him up in a magical prison for over 400 years.

WHAT'S UP!

Ireland's great. It's very green and breathtakingly beautiful. Driving has been a chore, but Bren acts like it's nothing. Whose bright idea was it to drive on the wrong side of the road! Anyway, we hit a few small towns that go back generations — but not his fam. Even found a Romany village. I really liked them. Those people know how to party. Anyway, we're going to try some of the smaller islands in the area. Hopefully, we'll have better luck there. Druid-quest continues. Looks like maybe another month here. I miss you so much, but it won't be for much longer.

Kiss Remy. Love ya much.

Leise

"I LIKE THAT part she put in for me," Remy said from over her shoulder.

She didn't jump, this ghost had been with her since she was a kid. "I bet you did. You might have to tell one of your girlfriends to help you out with that."

Remy's transparent body appeared next to her on the couch, where Nyah had been earlier. "I told you. I just enjoy their company. It's nice not being alone in Otherworld."

Otherworld is what they liked to call the magical realm inside of Leise's family heirloom. A rough-cut amethyst passed down through many generations of Morgan women. When used with the correct spell and a blood sacrifice, the magical world inside could become a prison.

"Haviland's there. You guys don't talk? Hangout?" Ari laughed when Remy growled. "I'll take that as a no."

"I've run into him occasionally. He really wants *her* there. You should go talk to him."

"I will. Soon. I promise." She knew she needed to visit him, but she didn't have any answers. Yes, they brought Nyah's spirit back from a nether realm which was much like purgatory; magical world created for souls. But instead of her spirit entering Otherworld to be with the love of her life, it found more suitable lodgings in one of the most recognizable, and recently deceased people in Houston.

"I hope so. It doesn't look like it did before. He was okay in the beginning, but now." His hands moved in a shaky pattern. "He might be losing it a little."

"Okay. I get it. I'll visit him, but it won't be tonight."

CHAPTER 2

Ari jumped out of Tiffany, her twenty-year-old light blue BMW, with her phone to her ear.

An automated voice said, "The mailbox is full. Try again, later. Good-bye." The line went dead.

Why weren't her cousins calling her back? It wasn't like Lucas or Rum not to return a call. Something must have happened. Nope. No. Don't even entertain that line of thinking, she told herself. They are just busy.

The gravel shuffled behind her. She kept walking but took a peek behind her. The tall man leaning against the dark sedan made her stop and fully turn around and walk in his direction.

Detective Adam Westin looked almost like a regular person in his jeans and dark t-shirt. He'd even let the buzz-cut grow out a bit. But nothing would change the way he stared at her. His honey-brown eyes felt like they could see right through her.

"Detective, the bar doors are in the front of the building," Ari said in a clipped tone.

"I know. Just stretching my legs," Westin said, still leaning against his car.

“What's your problem?”

"You want to know what my problem is?" He raised off the car door. "I know you did something to me, and I want to know what."

Ari shook her head. "I don't know what you're talking about."

Of course, she knew exactly what he was talking about, but she couldn't tell him that a witch nearly killed him, and she used a spell to heal him and take away his memory of that night. Nope. Not gonna happen. Besides, he wouldn't believe her if she did tell him.

His eyes squinted down so tight, she didn't think he could see her. "Whatever, you say." He leaned back on the car.

"If you didn't know, following me around like this is called stalking. I will be having a long conversation with your captain about it." She held up her phone and snapped a picture. "You should go home. Get some rest. You have bags under your eyes."

Ari walked backward away from him.

"This isn't over Mason!"

She lifted her hand with the phone in it and waved goodbye as she went to work.

Jacque, the new busboy, struggled to lift four crates of freshly washed glasses. His five-five frame disappeared behind the wobbly stack of glassware, leaving just his hands visible.

"Wait. Let me help you." She lifted one of the warm and still steaming plastic slated containers from the top of his load.

His head popped out from the side of the stack. "Th-Th-Thanks." He struggled to get out.

"No worries." She gave him a smile and a wink. There was something about Jacque she couldn't quite put her finger on. He brought a peaceful vibe anytime he came near her. She wondered what his aura would look like. The Cave, the building or the land it was built on, made it impossible to use her powers at all.

Jacque followed Ari out to the front bar area. She squeezed past her boss. When he lifted a brow, then looked at his watch, she slammed down the container and all the glasses rattled. She cringed and waited for it, but nothing shattered. Jacque put down his glasses with care, looked at them both, then scurried to the back.

"Don't say it, Bull. I already know." She grabbed a towel from the rack near the small sink and gingerly pulled a glass out to wipe it dry.

"What?" The big man hunched his shoulders. "All I was going to say was, happy you could join us." His smirk belittled the sincerity of his statement.

Ari couldn't help but smile back at him. Her boss stood seven-foot even with his boots on. He looked like a total bad-ass with his bald head and motorcycle club leather vest displaying two full colorful sleeves of tattoos up his arm, but listening to him giggle as he tried to keep a straight face revealed his true nature.

"Ain't that right, Jacque?" Bull said, as the busboy pushed out two large plastic containers of ice.

Jacque stopped in front of Ari.

"Is that correct, Jacque?" Her voice always softened when she spoke to him. A part of her felt like, between his speech impediment and shyness, he might not have gotten a lot of gentle in his life.

He looked between her and Bull. He turned back towards Ari and gave a shy smile and began to pour the ice into the metal bins. "Ye... yes, sir."

"See. Even Jacque was waiting." Bull's smile widened.

Ari knew Jacque was just agreeing to keep the peace and possibly his job. But over these last few months, she realized that was just how Jacque was. He had a stillness about him. Every once in a while, he carried true worry on him like a fur winter coat, but it never lasted long.

Ari smiled and said, "Fine, you're right. Sorry, I was late, Boss." She gave a small nod. "It will never happen again."

"Aw, hell. Ain't no need in lying."

They all laughed. Anyone who knew Ari knew she would probably show up late to her own funeral.

She lowered her voice and lifted her head towards the front of the bar. "Why are there people in here already?"

Bull didn't look away from the computer. "We opened fifteen minutes ago."

Yeah, yeah. "Did you get their order?"

"Um, no. I was waiting for the bartender-on-duty to handle that."

He could be such an ass sometimes. She rolled her eyes but said in a most genteel voice. "Getting right on it, Boss."

Ari wiped her hands on the drying rag before walking to the front of the seating area. The two people sat with their backs to the back, but her easy demeanor fell away as she reached them. She knew that long mane of curly red and black hair anywhere.

Her aunt.

"Tatum." Ari stopped next to the table. "What are you doing here?"

"You show her some respect!" The dark-haired young lady seated across from her aunt growled.

Tatum patted the table in front of the girl.

"But Lady Tatum, she—"

"Ella Grace." The older woman lifted her hand to stave off any further outbursts.

Much like a petulant child, Ella Grace slammed backward in her seat, with her lips pressed into a thin line, and her arms tightly bound across her nearly imperceptible chest.

Ari had never seen the *Wednesday Addams reject* before. She must have joined the coven after her own untimely departure a few years back.

"Aramais, this is a very interesting place you work at." The older woman couldn't disguise her disgust as she looked around the establishment. If she lifted her brows any higher, they'd be in her hairline.

"Speaking of work, some of us actually have a lot of it to do. So, I have to get back unless you want to order a drink."

"Fine. Two waters. Bottled."

Ari walked away, then quickly returned with the drinks. It took every bit of her control not to slam the bottles down, but in the end, she placed them down like a good waitress.

"Anything else?" Before her aunt or the girl could respond, she said, "Okay, fine." Then turned to leave, but before she got two steps away, her aunt spoke.

"Yes. Yes, there is."

Ari rolled her eyes before turning back around. She looked at her mother's sister and she was the epitome of what dismages—non-magical humans thought witches looked like. A black peasant top with a long, multi-colored maxi skirt, with large hoop earrings. Well, except for the moles, warts, and overall bad skin issues. That kind of thing was genetics. She had no intentions of being the old crone with a wart on the tip of her nose. She is a firm believer in eight glasses of water a day and a daily skincare regime. Just in case.

"The coven is having an All Hallows Eve celebration," Tatum answered.

Ari squinted her eyes at the statement. They wanted something. "Why now? It's been, what? Seven years?" You never asked me before went unsaid.

"The high priestess demands your presence."

Ari blinked, then blinked again. "Excuse me."

"You heard her," Ella Grace chimed in. Apparently keeping quiet no longer. "Your high priestess—"

"First of all," Ari's hand snapped up cutting her off, "I don't know you and second, she's not *my* high priestess."

Ella Grace jumped up, the chair hitting the floor from the force.

"You. Sit down." One red-polished fingernail pointed slowly from her, back to the chair.

"But."

"Not another word," Tatum clipped out.

Ari watched the girl pick up the chair and practically throw herself into it. Her eyes cut to the guys watching from the bar. "We're okay. She thought she saw something in the shadows," she said, with a smile. The smile fell away when she turned back.

"This is not a request," Tatum said brusquely.

"Look, I don't care what my mother wants. She and the Black Blood coven are no longer any concern of mine."

"Sorry to hear you say that." Tatum stood, and the girl stayed seated. "Come, Ella Grace." Only then did the girl get up.

If looks could kill, Ari would be dead on the spot. Instead of giving Ari a wide birth, the girl bumped her shoulder as she passed.

Ari's eyes burned from the geranium and rose oil the girl must have bathed in. One thing became crystal clear in that moment. Even in this bar where magical powers were often distorted, she should have felt some type of magical presence from that touch. There was nothing.

What is going on if her mother was allowing dismages into the coven?

CHAPTER 3

The thought of sleeping in her own bed filled Ari's mind as she pulled into her assigned parking spot on the far end of the lot. Between the need for being in her own space and plain, old exhaustion from dealing with drunken patrons all night, she wasn't on her game. All she needed was her memory-foam, cool gel pillow. That thing was magic in and of itself.

Goosebumps ran up both her arms as the cool night air flowed around her. The front doors of her building couldn't have been more than twenty-five feet away, but her mind was even further away. By the time she registered the needle-like pricks on her skin weren't goosebumps at all, but the dread that dark witches exuded before striking, it was nearly too late.

Ari turned in a circle holding her bag like a shield. Four people in black hooded robes. Something flew through the air and on instinct she blocked her body with her purse. The small bottle hit the leather, and it melted away in her hands.

What was that hell? That was a Fendi!

"Dammit, E.G. We were told to subdue her, not kill her," a hooded female said, from behind her.

Good to know they weren't there to kill her, but whatever was in that bottle would have messed her up pretty bad. E.G. was lucky she chose not to use blood magic like she'd been taught, they all would be dead already. That didn't stop her from launching three baseball-sized fireballs. Just enough to back the witches up.

The first fireball hit low, setting the petite witch's black robe on fire. What was it made of? Hemp? It caught fire so fast. Ari couldn't stop watching the fast-moving flames. One of the small corked bottles fastened to her hip hit the ground, and the flames kicked up higher.

As E.G. jumped around to put out the fire, the hood fell back revealing her face.

Ella Grace.

No matter how much she disliked the girl, she couldn't watch her burn to death. She was fighting to get away, not to murder someone. Before she could move to help the young witch; a fog of cold air consumed, then enveloped her. Putting the fire out and leaving flecks of ice crystals on the young girl's robe.

"Dumb witch." Ari heard a male grumble with a slight accent. She wasn't sure if he was referring to her or the partially frozen witch on the ground.

"Look," Ari said, looking around to the three remaining hooded witches. "I think you guys have the wrong person."

"No, Princess Aramais Mason. We do not," another robed male said.

Before she could say anything else, they all seemed to move at once. *Where was that blue spirit flame when she needed it?*

Her eyes couldn't keep up with the person in front of her. Was this person actually moving that fast? The robe billowed behind him. When the figure would appear before her, she'd throw a fire-ball, then poof. Gone. That happened a few times until she just started throwing fire in every direction hoping to just graze any of them.

"Stop playing with her and end this," the female voice said with a growl.

The three billowing robed figures stopped moving. The middle figure tilted his hooded head to one side, stretched out his hands and the two figures on both sides of him dissipated, like sands in the wind, disappearing into the palms of his hands.

Ari hadn't blinked, but she knew what she just saw. What type of magic was that? Did he create clones? Out of sand or dirt? She didn't want to be in awe of a bad guy, but in a way, that was awesome.

Before she could mentally praise this witch anymore, she slapped at the stinging sensation on her neck. It felt like a mosquito, but instantly she knew better. A wave of nausea rolled up through her.

She blinked as she looked around. Her building kept going in and out of focus, no matter how many times she tried to clear the fogginess away. When she would have fallen, a huge hand fastened around her forearm, holding her up.

"Easy, Princess," he said near her ear.

The male's lightly accented, deep baritone voice rumbled through her. The accent had hints of an Asian influence, but she couldn't place it exactly. He was the one with the cold or freezing ability. Her mind wasn't a complete foggy town.

"Why are you doing this to me?" Ari wasn't sure if she said this aloud or was still chit-chatting in her own head. She finally stopped blinking and let her eyes stay closed.

"She wants to see you," the female said.

'She.' Ari's mind grasped at that one word for a moment and then it clicked. Slowly, but it came to her. Only one person would go to these extremes. "Most people called or texted." *My mother is such a bit—*. She couldn't hold together the rest of the thought.

"At least she cares enough to see you."

Ari didn't understand why he'd said that, but it took too much brainpower to think it through. She let go and her world went black.

CHAPTER 4

"Is she dead?"

Ari recognized that voice. She tried not to sneeze as Ella Grace's scent wafted all around her. Geranium and roses oil weren't her favorite scents, and together, it was more than her poor nose could take. The girl smelled too much like a citronella candle. She'd been awake for only a short time but heard the unending tirade.

"I don't know why the high priestess wants her so bad. She's nothing special."

Ari wanted to roll her eyes. This girl was brimming with jealousy. But why, she didn't even know her.

"And she's not even pretty," Ella Grace said with a petulant huff.

"Ella Grace. Enough," a male voice growled.

"Leaves, why are you taking up for her. You think she's pretty or something?"

The girl said it in a way that Ari suspected that 'Leaves' wasn't his real name. A crackle of freezing air whooshed over Ari. It took everything in her not to jump up and scream bloody murder.

The girl, however, yelled, "Why are you always so mean to me?"

"Why do you insist on calling me that name?"

"I like it."

Ari could also hear the words she didn't say. *I like you.*

"Go away," he growled.

"Fine." A few moments later, the door slammed.

Interesting. Ari waited a heartbeat, maybe even two before she cracked open an eye. She expected to be in a cell or basement. Despite the room's stark appearance and bare walls, the only coldness she'd felt came from the corner behind her.

From him. From Leaves.

She wondered if she called him that name would she get the same reaction. With great trepidation, her feet moved to the floor, and she sat up. There wasn't a window, or clock or anything to indicate how long she'd been out.

For a windowless, tasteless room, the carpet felt like heaven. The dark gray fibers cushioned her feet as they sank in as she wiggled her toes. She then stood up, "Oh, my." She grabbed her head and sat back down. A mountain-sized headache came out of nowhere.

"Not a good move, Princess."

A deep accented voice grumbled from behind her. Ari lifted her hand, poised to throw a fireball. Nothing. Before she could really assess why her powers weren't working, a sharp pain rendered her partially blind for a moment and all she could do was cradle her closed eyes.

"One, I'm not a princess and two, what did you do to me?"

"Whatever you say, Princess. Magic dampeners. Word is you have some weird super firepower."

How could they know about that? Is her mother keeping tabs on her? She rarely used her powers and they couldn't possibly know about her new power? Could they?

Her mother had ordered the witches in the Research and Development branch of the coven to work on magic dampeners when she was a kid, but they never really got it to work. They were having issues tailoring the potion to a witch's special power, and they scrapped the project. Guess they sorted that out since she left.

"Just like this room." He waved one hand around flippantly. "You can't say spells in here."

They really wanted to make sure she didn't burn the house

down. The room didn't look like one she'd been in before. But she could feel a rumbling through the walls, that could be cars. She might be still in the city. At least they didn't drag her out to the cabin. That place was at least two hours away, deep in the woods.

Once the throbbing stopped and her blindness cleared, she turned to look at him. His black leather loafers were propped up on a large ceramic planter. His dark gray suit jacket laid folded neatly over a chair next to him. The sleeves of his crisp, light gray shirt were rolled slightly up his arms like he'd been there a while.

She leaned forward like that would help her see under his straight bone-white hair that hung well past his shoulders. "Excuse me."

His fingers ran through his hair, pushing it back from his face, revealing strong Asian features with crystalline blue eyes in a thin, chiseled face. "Yes."

Ari's eyes were still on his lips when he answered. She had too much pride to shake herself, but took a deep breath before asking, "Why did you kidnap me?"

"A kidnapping would mean you're a child. And Princess, you're no little girl." There was a glimmer in his eyes when he said the last, before his hair hid him away again.

"I'm not a princess," Ari said, with a growl. She was sure she heard him laugh her. "Okay, why did you abduct me then?"

"Not an abduction."

"What do you call it when four witches grab a girl off the street, drug her, and take her against her will to goddess knows where?" Ari waved her hand around the room.

He lifted his head. "Facilitating a family meeting."

Ari opened her mouth to continue their tête-à-tête, when he lifted one finger to halt whatever she was about to say. He lifted a cellphone to his ear but didn't talk, mostly grunted. When he ended the call, he stood up, rolled down his sleeves before sliding into his suit jacket. His tall, muscular frame didn't seem to waste any movements.

"It's time."

The grumbly voice had returned, along with the abruptness

when he answered. Guess social hour was over. "I'm not going anywhere." She crossed her arms over her chest. She felt like a grouchy kid, and she knew it, but he'd given her no reason to follow him.

As she'd looked up, and up, and up towards his face. She didn't remember him being so tall. She could tell he was Asian by the gentle curve of his eyes and thin build, but there had to be some Nordic branches in his family tree due to his height. His light blue eyes bored into hers and with the steady thump going on in her head she couldn't win their stare contest. She closed her eyes and took a deep breath to stave off the drum solo banging in her head.

"Look," she paused, but when he said nothing, she continued, "look, Buddy. You've abducted me and jacked with my powers. I'm not sure what type of side effects that magic dampener thingy will have, and my head is killing me. Why on earth do you think I would willingly go anywhere with you? Let alone deal with my mother." Her little soap-box moment didn't help her headache to which was becoming a full-blown migraine at this point.

"I can't do anything about the past, but I might be able to fix your headache. Can you stand?"

When she didn't move, he extended his hand. The throbbing and pulsing overruled her stubbornness. She scooted to the edge of the sofa before pushing up. She tried to do it slowly, but the entire room tilted. She wobbled, but his strong hands grabbed her by the waist, stopping her imminent face-plant.

His powerful hands guided her backward. "Okay. Maybe, you should sit."

Her need to roll her eyes was tempered by the sharp pain behind them at the same-exact moment and she complied.

"Close your eyes." His face didn't give away anything as he squatted down before her.

Without question, she closed her lids. Acquiescence went against her nature, but the migraine was killing her, and she didn't want to die here.

The air around her became cooler as he invaded her personal space. She nearly jumped out of her skin when the pads of his fingers touched her temples. They were like little ice cubes pressed against her skull. He stopped moving. She exhaled what she only imagined being a long stream of cool smoke; it wasn't, but in her mind, she felt like she'd stepped out into the snowy tundra.

"You okay?" He continued after she wiggled in her spot, to get comfortable and nodded.

His fingers moved in a slow, circular motion. His power entered her head in crisp ripples, then flowed through her entire body with invigorating pulses. Her body drew taut as a bowstring with his power, then the last burst of his cold energy pushed her over the edge. A loud groan that sounded too much like a moan of passion filled the room. A bone deep shiver cascaded from the follicles of her freshly dyed purple hair to the tips of her newly French manicured toenails.

His fingers moved behind her ears, down her neck, then the surprising warmth of his breath breezed over her cheek. He'd leaned in as his magical hands worked around to the base of her head, down her spine. At that point, she was putty in his hands.

Ari wasn't sure if he went to massage school or learned the art of the Kama Sutra from a master, but if he could do this to her with two fingers, she could only imagine what he could do with his entire body.

When he removed his hands completely, her body slumped from the loss. Or was that relief? Knowing that she could and would do anything he asked of her as long as he kept touching her, sobered her right up.

"Better?"

Like coming out of a deep, revitalizing sleep, she blinked her eyes open. "Yes." The word came out sultrier than she'd intended. She cleared her throat and tried again. "Thank you."

Something about him made her look up and his eyes drew her in. They seemed to go from a clear blue to a stormy gray the longer they held each other's gazes. This man had a deep well of magic he'd yet to tap into. He came off as a bit arrogant and a lot of *I don't care about anything*, but his aura vibrated with the power of a high priest. She should know, her mother was the high priestess.

His magic must have jump-started hers. For the first time since they hit her with that dart, her fingertips tingled with power. Her hand moved of their own volition. He didn't move, and she didn't stop. She wanted to touch him, taste him. Tap into that power that he'd secreted away.

A voice from the door broke the intensity flowing between them. "Leif."

They both blinked and shook their heads like they were coming out of a spell. Leif stepped back and held his hand out to her.

"She's coming."

CHAPTER 5

"Hello." A leggy young lady greeted Ari with a stiff outstretched arm and rigid smile.

Ari had only caught a glimpse of her surroundings before her hand was clasped in a vice-like grip. The dress with the wide lace collar and navy tea-length dress was a nice 50s replica, but the brunette had a kung-fu grip that would rival G.I. Joe's.

"I'm Blythe." She curtsied with a slight head bow once she released Ari's hand. Black crinoline peeked from under the hem. "Nice to meet you. We weren't sure if you would make it today." Her Louisiana accent ran through every word.

Ari's eyes widened. "Really?" That shocked the hell out of her. "Well, I didn't know I was expected."

She looked behind her. Leif stood next to the man who called them out of the room. She suspected he was part of the guard, but he didn't look like he could protect much. He reminded her more of a kindergarten teacher with his tortoise-shell round glasses and clean-cut hairstyle. The weapon at his waist resembled an open-faced 9 mm dart gun. That told her all she needed to know.

Leif and the guard looked straight ahead unflinchingly. If she were a betting woman, she was sure an automaton had more personality than both of them at this moment. So much for asking what the heck was going on. The young lady's voice snapped Ari out of her daydream.

"Yes, my lady," Blythe said, before extending her hand in an usher like fashion. "Please come with me."

The room's spell clung to her. She didn't notice it so much while she was inside but now that she'd walked a few feet from the door it held her taut, before snapping back like a rubber band. Ari exhaled a sigh of relief. And just like that, her memories and thoughts were clear as a bell. That room's spell made it difficult to think.

She kept in step with Blythe. Leif and his robotic sidekick tagged along behind them. "Is that a bit of NOLA I hear?" It was like listening to Remy.

Blythe's reserved manner melted and revealed the real person underneath. "Why, yes. Yes, it is." Her smile didn't disappear like before. Then she nodded like she'd just decided something important. "You are not what I expected."

"I hope that's a good thing?"

Blythe didn't say anything more, just gave a tight smile. That told Ari all that she needed to know.

"It's okay. I know how everyone feels about me in this coven." She just didn't realize any of the stories had left Texas.

Of course, Ari didn't want to see her mother but she would do whatever she needed to, to get out of this prison. They walked in silence upstairs. The halls were filled with people Ari had never seen before. When she was a child, only Black Blood witches could walk the halls. Back then she knew everyone. Today, she only recognized one or two faces.

When they reached the main floor, Blythe waited for the gang of squealing teenage witches to walk by. "They say that you turned your back on your coven, denounced your powers, and became a...," she cut her eyes to Ari, "a tarot card reader in the park. But mostly, I heard that you were a bitch."

Ari lifted her brows at Blythe. "Tell me how you really feel then." She wasn't mad, just shocked a stranger had even heard of her, let alone in such detail.

"No, No," Blythe flushed. "That's what I heard, but having met you, I can tell that some of that might have been an exaggeration."

"The truth is, I am a tarot reader in the park and occasionally, I can be a bitch," Ari said, then smiled. Especially after being snatched off the streets and dragged here.

The corners of Blythe's mouth quirked up as she unsuccessfully held back a smile.

Ari felt like this was the real Blythe. A happy girl trapped by the confines and rules of her coven. "What's going on tonight?"

"I'm not really sure. I've heard talk though."

Ari watched as the still dark blue aura of uncertainty circled Blythe.

"Our covens...," Blythe paused like she was carefully choosing her words, "well, after tonight. Everything will change."

Ari didn't have to read the woman's aura to see her body sigh in relief. Whatever was happening, Blythe wanted it to happen. They continued in silence to their destination. When they arrived, Blythe opened the door, then stood to the side.

Ari nodded to Blythe, then looked past her towards Leif. Their eyes met for a brief moment before she turned into the unknown. Blythe gave her a stiff nod, then hurriedly closed the door behind her.

'Everything will change?' *What did that mean and what did it have to do with her?*

She stood in the middle of her mother's office. The large high-backed leather chair behind the mahogany desk slowly swiveled around to reveal a fair-skinned woman dressed in all white with salt and pepper hair tied into a tight bun.

Erissa Mason.

Her mother leaned forward, then steepled her fingers. "Blessed be, Aramais Delphine. So happy you could join us."

Ari cringed at the use of her entire name. Her mother never would just call her the nickname her father gave her as a child. Before she could correct the high priestess, people she'd recognized from her old coven poured in behind the oversized desk, surrounding her mother. Not that she needed it.

Noise filled the room, Ari turned to see the doors open behind her and more people poured into the room. This must be Blythe's coven. Ari turned enough to keep her eyes on both covens. Judging by the cut of the Armani suits on the men and Manolos and mink stole on the apparent matriarch, this clan had money.

What version of hell had she just stepped into?

"Erissa." Ari looked around the room. "I didn't realize this would be a community meeting. Now, can you tell me why the hell I'm here?"

"She is so disrespectful." A female voice whispered from the back of the other coven.

Ari's body stiffened, but she fought the urge to stare down the crowd looking for the culprit. Her eyes stayed steady on her mother. The woman's magical attacks were faster than a pit viper. This was why Ari trained to perform her magic without the use of blood or a wand. She could never best her mother during training.

"Aramais, I would like for you to meet..." Erissa started.

"Cut the BS." Ari cut in. "Why am I here?"

"Petulant child," her mother mumbled. "Fine," Erissa said louder. "They are here to discuss your engagement." A hand waved nonchalantly toward the other coven.

Ari's knees buckled. She wanted to sit or fall, whichever was faster after hearing that tidbit of news. There were too many enemies around her to take a seat. "Um, excuse me?"

"You heard me. Now, let's discuss your impending nuptials." Erissa continued.

"I'm not marrying anyone. Hell, I'm not even a part of this coven." She turned fully towards her mother now.

"That can be easily rectified."

"No, it can't. Because I don't want any part of this coven or whatever," she waved around the room, "this carnival show you got going on here."

"It has already been decided," Erissa said seemingly unaffected by Ari's outburst.

Ari could hear the, *Whether you want to or not*, in her mother's statement but responded nonetheless. "What do you get out of this?"

Erissa blinked like she was taken aback. "Excuse me."

“You heard me. What? Money? More control?" Ari wave towards the other group. Rumbles had begun in their camp. "What's wrong with him?"

The well-dressed matriarch sputtered. "Excuse me. There's nothing wrong with my son." She flipped her mink stole over her shoulder. "You need to get control of your daughter." Her eyes flared towards Erissa.

"There has to be." Ari moved into the haughty woman's direction. "Look at you. Dressed to the nines. This is a holey jeans and t-shirt coven, at best. Your son should be able to marry anyone. Unless..." Ari lifted her brows with a smirk. Leaving the statement out there.

The woman turned a bright red. Embarrassment was the tip of the iceberg. Deep blue eyes glaring; she was enraged. The wedding should be called off any minute now.

Preparing for a quick exit, Ari backed up, but two men blocked the doors. One was over six-feet tall and clean-shaven, the other a few inches shorter, bald with a full reddish-brown beard. Both in black suits with dark blue shirts and ties.

"Aramais. No more of your childish games," Erissa said.

"Games." Ari snatched her arm away before Reddish Beard could grab and stop her. "I will not be your sacrificial lamb."

"It's for the good of the coven," Erissa said with grace and calm.

Ari could have been asking the time for all the feeling she put into the words. Her voice did not reflect any modicum of calm. "I'm not part of the coven or did you forget?" A rhetorical question.

Erissa moved in front of Ari. "You will do as you're told, child."

"Or what? You can't make me." Ari moved closer to her mother. Practically daring the woman to try.

"Smitty. Subdue her," Erissa said with the flip of her hand.

Reddish Beard moved his hand towards the 9mm gun with pink liquid-filled darts.

Magic dampeners.

"Dilapsus putrefacio," Ari yelled with hands outstretched, before he fired at her.

The gun began to melt in his hand. Covered in molten metal, his hand, then forearm melted away. Smitty fell to the floor howling in pain, holding his nub of an arm. Ari looked away as the curse consumed his arm. When the room went eerie quiet, and only Smitty's screams filled the room.

"Aramais. He was my best guard. Pity." Erissa looked behind her. "Someone get him out of here."

Two young men carried Smitty out of the room. Erissa pulled one of the jade and labradorite chopsticks from her hair, then flattened her hair back into place. "I can't have you doing that again though." She flicked the chopstick. "Comprimere."

Ari's head whipped back from the force of the silence curse.

"Levis subvolo suppateo." Erissa continued with the wave of her wand.

Ari's arms snapped back like rubber-bands when she tried to pull against the binding spell. She closed her eyes to concentrate on what to do, but her body jerked as she floated a few feet in the air.

The witches in the room wouldn't help her. Not that she expected them to. A few of the lesser witches ran out the door. In a magical battle, no one could interfere. At least, that's how it used to be. She didn't know the rules in this new world her mother had created.

"Aramais Delphine Mason," Erissa said.

Ari's eyes opened wide. When a witch's full name is used in a spell, it worked like a compulsion spell. She struggled against it, but it was futile.

"You will learn to do as you're told." Erissa took the end the wand, twisted, and the glint of metal rotated out of the body of the wand. Ari shook her head emphatically, but the spell held, and no one could hear her scream. The blade sliced into Ari's arm.

Drops of blood hit the floor as the curse coursed through her veins. Ari closed her eyes and concentrated on the fire deep in her soul. She thought of blue flames.

The spirit flame.

Ari didn't really know how to control her new power, but all she could concentrate on was burning this curse out of her body. Needing to be free of her mother's control. She focused on the heat deep within her core, much like how she created flames in her hands, she pushed the thought throughout her entire body.

"You will do as I say, from this point on." Erissa continued to cut runes into Ari's arm. "Or that best friend of yours might need to disappear. Maybe all those old dismages you care so much about should happen to go insane. Old people are so fragile. Their minds can just," she snapped her fingers, "snap."

For the first time in two months, she was happy Leise was out of the country.

A sizzling sensation burned across her lips freeing them. "I can't let you hurt them."

Her mother's surprise was nearly comical. Erissa stepped back slowly. "You shouldn't be able to do that."

"You will never control me!" Ari's body jerked from the force of spirit flame as it burned through her entire body. Then a blue light flared from her hands and mouth. The light was so intense it blinded her, and made her ears pop right before her entire body collapsed onto the floor.

Ari heaved to catch her breath. Every person still in the room gaped and gawked at her. She could see her mother's mouth moving but she couldn't hear a word as she staggered to her feet.

Erissa held her hand out towards her like she was trying to coax a wild animal back into its cage. Ari knew her mother was up to something. How did she know? The woman was smiling.

Her hearing came back online just as her mother said, "I am your mother. I would never hurt you."

Ari's eyes went wide just as Erissa poised her wand to strike. She began the spell, but before she could finish, Ari whipped out her hand. Unlike her mother, she didn't need to say a spell out loud or use a wand for it to work. Ari extended the fingers wide on her right hand, then pushed outward forcefully, then snatched it back into a tight ball.

Erissa toppled over. The people in the room took a step back from the two. She lifted her hand and Erissa's body slowly rose until her feet dangled.

"Mother, just because I choose not to use my magic to hurt people," she lifted her hand and her mother rose higher, "doesn't mean I won't."

"You surprise me, daughter," Erissa gasped out.

"I don't care." She swung her mom's body to the opposite wall against the floor to ceiling bookshelves. Books fell and witches ran over each other to get out of the way. "You cannot keep me here and I will marry no one until I'm good and damn ready."

She looked at the matriarch of the other coven. "Whatever she promised you, it's not worth it." She expected the woman to be horrified, but instead, the woman looked at her with such avarice. It was almost scary.

She turned her attention back towards her mother who was still suspended in the air. "I'm leaving. Don't contact me again and this whole marriage," she looked at the crowd at large shaking her head, "not happening."

Erissa groaned out. "You are stronger than I—"

"Enough!" Ari shouted.

Erissa's mouth became a tight line. Although her mother's jaw moved, her lips never parted. Sealed shut. It was a pity this curse was temporary. But she was sure the entire coven could do with a day of silence.

Ari turned back towards the room. "I'm done here."

The guards still blocked the door.

Ari closed her eyes like she was tired but spoke when she opened them. "You really don't want me to move you." She lifted a brow when they didn't move initially.

They looked past her towards the other coven, then stepped aside. She didn't care who okayed her leaving, she just needed to get out. Her body bristled with the energy of her rarely used power. It felt like a cauldron of molten lava overflowing from her toes to the tips of her unflattering split ends.

She waved her hand behind her and heard her mother's body hit the floor.

Ari couldn't remember how she made it outside. Her legs were limp as noodles as she staggered out of the coven townhouse. She remembered fresh air, city noise, a pair of strong arms catching her, and comforting words whispered in her ear.

"I got you, Princess."

CHAPTER 6

The enticing aroma of cooking chicken roused Ari from a deep sleep. Was Nyah trying to use the microwave again? *Nyah.* She jumped up. *Cooking?!* The silk sheets slipped to her waist. *Black silk. Four poster bed made for a king-sized man.* She looked over the side. Was that a dais? And shag carpet? This was not her room. Where was she?

It might have taken a minute for it all to come rushing back. Her mother and the fight at the Black Blood coven townhouse. She'd used her new power and passed out. She flung the covers back just as Leif opened the door. That delicious scent preceded him as he walked in .

"Good. You're finally awake." He stood next to the bed. When she didn't move, he lifted his brows with a head lift.

"Oh." She scooted back in the bed, pulling the sheet over her lap. He placed a standing tray with a bowl of food and a glass of orange juice over her legs, then he sat next to her.

"How do you feel?"

"How do you think I feel? You've abducted me." She flinched, squinting her eyes. Her headache made her use her inside voice. "Again."

"The first time was business." He held the glass of orange juice out to her. She just looked at it. He took a sip, then held it back out to her, only then did she take it. "This time, I saved you."

She turned the glass away from where his lips touched, then sipped the juice. "How do you figure?"

"You would have hit the pavement without me. Maybe got a nasty bruise on the back of your head. Who knows, you could've even gotten a concussion. Speaking of which, I'll be right back."

He walked into the small adjacent room. The bathroom.

When he returned, he held out his fist to her. "Take these." Then dropped two white aspirin into her hand. She would normally drink a special blend of pain powder made from herbs, but this was an emergency. She popped the pills into her mouth and took two big gulps of O.J. to wash them down.

"Please eat. My mom always made this for breakfast when I wasn't feeling good."

She looked at the enticing bowl but didn't move to eat any. He looked annoyed, but reached for her spoon, and consumed a mouthful. He lifted his brows in a "see" gesture.

"Can you blame me? You did kidnap me." She used the napkin to clean the spoon.

"Rescued," he countered.

"That's debatable." She sort of thought she saved herself all the way up to the point where she fainted. "So, um, your mom made you chicken soup for breakfast?" The ceramic pot was considerably bigger than a bowl. There was no way she could eat all of it.

"It's called Dakjuk. A Korean chicken porridge, it can be eaten anytime, really."

Ari scooped out a small spoonful and could see it was much more than a soup. It was a thick broth-like stew, with bits of chicken, julienned carrots, chopped green onions, and rice. She blew on it before taking a tentative taste. Her mouth blossomed with full, robust flavors. She dug in after that.

"Your mom taught you how to make this?" She asked between spoonfuls.

He nodded.

"Well, thank her for me. It's delicious."

He gave a small nod. But in the light of day, his aura went from golden to deep blue in a snap. Sadness was a third person in the room with them. Before she knew it, Ari had eaten the entire pot. She leaned back against the headboard, patting her stomach.

"I guess I was hungry."

"Guess so." The corner of his mouth quirked up as he took the tray and walked out of the room.

Ari closed her eyes. A familiar chill flowed over her. When she opened her eyes, they met those of her best friend.

"Remy?" She looked at the door, then back to him as she quickly rose. "Where have you been?"

"I could sense you, but I couldn't find you," Remy chided.

Damn wards. Ari nodded then asked, "What are you doing here? Did she burn down my apartment?"

He floated to his feet then casually looked around the room. As if he were shopping. Ari was sure if he could touch anything, he would be checking jewelry and paintings to see if they were fake. "So, this where you were all night? I thought you took her out to a movie or something. She wasn't home last night either."

"What? You sure?" She told Nyah not to go outside out of fear of someone recognizing her. But she was a grown woman and had to be bored out of her mind. "Is she home, now?"

"Last I saw, she was attempting the make breakfast."

"What?!" Ari hopped out of the bed, then wobbled on her feet. A strong arm stopped her from hitting the floor.

"I'm okay." She held her hands out as if to balance herself, and took few deep breaths. "Yeah, I'm good."

Leif held his hands up. "Where are you going?"

"I need to get home. Where are my shoes?"

A doorbell rang. "Wait. I'll drive you home."

"I can catch an Uber."

A light knock, then a female's voice called his name.

He held up a finger. "One minute."

Of course, she was curious what type of woman the mysterious Leif was in to, but she couldn't see into the living room from the bedroom. It only took a minute to realize who it was though. Between that voice and the geranium/rose oil concoction, Ella Grace could not be mistaken for anyone else.

Ari couldn't really hear and frankly didn't want to hear anything that little witch wannabe had to say. As she looked around for her shoes, a well-known chilliness flowed over her preceding her best friend's arrival.

"You want me to listen in for you?" Remy followed next to her.

"No," she hissed.

"You sure about that?" Remy's smile could rival the Cheshire cat.

She eyed him but didn't utter another word.

"Okay, okay, Cher." He waved quickly. "I was trying to aide a woman in need."

"I'm perfectly fine." She opened the closet door. "I just need to find my shoes."

Ari wasn't sure if his clothing options surprised her or not. Suits and lots of them. A variety of styles and name brands, but not a huge selection of colors. The jackets spanned in an ombré of colors from the deepest blues, through shades of gray, to the brightest whites. Her fingers gently grazed the material as she looked at each vest. A three-piece suit had to be the sexiest piece of equipment a man could possess. But in this Texas heat, it was rare to see, if ever.

A throat cleared behind her. She nearly jumped out of her skin.

“Find what you're looking for in there?”

“Actually, no. Where are my—?”

He held them out to her before she finished her sentence. She gave a polite smile as she took them. “Thank you.”

She knew it was none of her business. Even swore she would keep her nose out of it, but she had to know. After she took a seat on the light-colored wooden bench near the window to put on her shoes, the words just came out. “So, Ella Grace and—”

A firm "No" resounded before she could get the rest out.

"You are aware that she likes you, and dare I say, in love with you?"

"She's a kid."

That didn't answer the question. "You aren't much older than her."

His voice seemed to drop an octave. "I'm twenty-eight years old."

Ari stopped tying her shoe and her brows lifted, then she blinked a few times.

"Don't look so surprised," he mumbled under his breath.

For an instant, she could see the petulant youth he must have been. And gloried in the handsome man he'd become. "You come from good genes; I can't fault you for that."

"Let me use your phone."

"Why?" He walked out of the room. She followed, hot on his heels.

"Don't be like this. Just—" Be a good guy, she thought.

He jingled his keys. "Just what? I told you I would drive you, now let's go."

This man was proving to be better than some self-proclaimed *good guys* she knew.

CHAPTER 7

Ari walked into a smoke-free apartment. "Hello? Nyah? Remy? Anyone home?"

"Roommates?"

Ari looked behind her. "Why are you following me?"

When Leif didn't answer, she moved further into her place. "I thought I told you I was fine, and you didn't need to come up. My wards could incinerate you, just FYI."

The magical security system had been deactivated the moment she touched the door, but he didn't need to know that.

Leif let out a grunt of a laugh, but in her periphery, she saw that he'd stopped moving. That didn't keep him from looking around the living room though. Good. She checked the kitchen; it looked normal. A mess. Dirty plates and bowls in the sink. But no burned pots. Not being able to master the microwave, Nyah had been cooking over an open fire on the stove. Ari wouldn't let her near a BBQ grill without supervision.

"Aria, is that you?" A muffled voice called out.

"Yeah," Ari said from the open balcony sliding door.

As she stepped back into the living room, it dawned on her too late Nyah's aversion to wearing clothes. They argued about the necessity to cover up *all* of her body parts and finally agreed that before bed she could be mostly in her natural state. She rushed to the hallway just in time to see too much but not in time to stop it. A towel covered Nyah's head and not much else. She could only imagine how much Leif saw before she turned him around.

"Nyah, don't—" *come out.* The words died when Nyah released a scream that harkened closer to nails on a blackboard, then feet pounded down the hall.

Leif looked behind him with a devilish grin. "The roommate, I presume."

Ari turned his head away from Nyah's bare bottom as she pushed him towards the entrance. "Yeah, time for you to go." He'd seen far too much.

Leif stood in the hallway. "You are a most interesting creature, Princess. Until next time."

"Not if I can help it." She planted on a fake smile as she closed the door in his face.

"Nyah. He's gone. You can come out now. And..." Ari sat on the sofa and waited.

Nyah stepped out in a long white ribbed t-shirt still with the towel in her hands. Ari patted a spot next to her on the couch.

"Who was that?" Nyah asked softly.

Ari waved her hand dismissively. "No one important. What happened to your hair?" She touched the tip of the young woman's pale, damp hair.

"I've been watching the picture box." She pointed towards the television. "The magic of this time is wondrous. You can change your eye color, hair color, even skin can be lightened or darkened."

"How did you?" She lifted her hand towards the wavy mane.

"Oh." Nyah jumped up and ran out of the room. She returned holding a box. "There were so many. But you do everything with herbs, so I got this one." She handed a green box of hair color with sprigs of herbs and an avocado seed with oil around it - Light Golden Blonde.

"I used the green paper. The money. Do you think people will still think I am her?" She touched her neck nervously.

Ari really looked her over. The hair color helped, but those long, wavy tresses might be a giveaway no matter what. "Maybe a little trim."

Nyah nodded enthusiastically.

Thirty minutes later, a few inches shorter and some bangs later, Nyah didn't look exactly like Royal.

Ari watched as Nyah looked at herself in the bathroom mirror as she ran her fingers through the shorter hairstyle. "I like it. Thank you. I think I am ready to see Haviland."

"You know, you will look like yourself and not this body in that world?"

She nodded, "I know. But I have decided. I want to help people… like you."

They walked back to the living room and sat down. "I was always ill. My legs and arms weren't strong. I couldn't do anything in our tribe. But here... I can change the world. But I should say goodbye to Hav first."

Ari nodded. "I'll call Buster and get some items together."

"Buster, he's the one who helped you bring me back, yes?"

"Yes. He's not a witch, but he knows a lot about spells and performing rituals."

Nyah's smile widened. "I would like to show my gratitude. I feel like I already know him."

"I couldn't have helped you without him."

Nyah picked at invisible lint on her shirt. "Can I ask you something?"

"You know you can," Ari said.

"The guy. He was cute. Is he your mate?"

"Goddess, no." Ari shook her head. "He's what we call, trouble."

Buster leaned forward in a graceful stretch, his long dreadlocks flopped forward as his arms extended wide, then flowed towards the floor into a downward dog position. A chill ran up his spine and his eyes popped open.

Something or a bunch of somethings were testing his protection wards again. He heard a light pop when the spirit squeezed through his magical security system. This was something small, not powerful enough to break through his wards, but tiny enough to get in. Souls, spirits, ghosts - whatever you want to call them, they were circling his place like a pack of hyenas waiting on a juicy steak.

Instead of trying to possess him, the little spirit put a cold hand on his shoulder, cupped Buster's ear, and whispered a secret. Buster quickly picked up the phone and made a call.

"Ari." Buster's thick Jamaican accent made her name sound like 'Air-Ree'. "Is everything going okay wit cha?"

"Were your ears burning? We were just talking about you. I was going to call you in the morning," Ari said with a laugh in her voice.

"About what?"

"Nyah. She's ready."

His eyes widened. "Wow. Is she really going to stay with him?"

"Who knows? I certainly hope so. That's why I'm calling. I could really use your help."

"I don't know. Things have been crazy around here." He walked as far as the coiled phone cord would allow around the room with his hand out. Feeling for cold spots along the walls. "The spirit realm is excited about something."

"I always see a lot more of them this time of year," Ari said.

"I forget you can see ghosts. Well, they have been busy around here. I had to double my wards." He knew something had been brewing in the supernatural world for more than a month. The spirits had been particularly vocal without him having to summon them.

"Do I need to make you something so you can leave safely?"

Ari sounded concerned. His heart filled with joy to know he had a friend who understood and cared about him. He met Ari under the most difficult of circumstances — losing his best friend to a murderous witch. But he was happy they found each other.

"I got it covered for now, but I might need something stronger.

I'll need to pick up some supplies. Is that devilish Detective Westin still on your tail?"

"I should hope not. I had to call his superiors. After a short conversation about stalking, police harassment, and me filing charges, I haven't seen him for a while. Although, I could have used him the other night," she said the last wistfully.

"Why? What happened?"

"Nothing much. A family reunion."

"Oh."

He'd heard tales of Ari's family. The Black Blood coven used blood magic to gain power and fortune. They were nothing less than mercenaries. Ari was too good for them in more ways than one.

"How's midnight tomorrow?"

"What? Oh, no, Honey chil', I have a date. We doing this thing early, more like 10:30. I can't be hanging out with you girls all night."

They both laughed before she spoke again. "Understood. It shouldn't take too long."

CHAPTER 8

The thin sliver of the moon hung in the cloudless sky. Ari had prepped her bag with two flashlights. The waning moon wasn't going to put out much light tonight. A car was already parked around the block from the cemetery when she pulled up.

"He's here already. He must really want to be on time for that date." Ari said to Nyah as they got out of Tiffany. "Grab that bag." She pointed towards the back seat, then grabbed her messenger bag and a flashlight.

"Ladies," Buster said when he got out of his small two-seater. "Nice of you to make it."

Ari looked at her watch. "You're just early. Buster, I'd like for you to meet—" she looked to her left, then right, then finally turned all the way around.

Nyah had positioned herself completely out of Buster's view, directly behind Ari with her head down.

"Girl, what are you doing?" She whispered with her back towards Buster. "He's okay, I promise. You can trust him. Now, if you've changed—"

"No," Nyah interjected softly, but forcefully.

"Are you ready?" When she nodded, Ari interlaced her fingers with Nyah's and pulled her closer to Buster.

"Buster, this is Nyah."

"I presumed as much," he said with a smile. "Nice to meet you." He held out his hand.

Nyah looked at the hand, Buster, then Ari. "I, um," she stammered.

"Just reach out, like I showed you." Ari motioned her hand and moved it in an up and down motion, then smiled. "They didn't…" she said to Buster.

"Shake hands in her time. Yeah, I've been doing some research," he finished for her.

"Nice to meet you, Nyah," he said, when her palm finally met his.

Ari stood back waiting for the earth-shaking jolt between them like when Buster first met her. But nothing. Buster gave an easy smile, released Nyah's hand, then slung his man bag over his shoulder.

"You ladies ready for a little B&E?"

"What's a 'B and E'?" Nyah leaned into Ari and whispered.

"It means breaking and entering a property that you don't own, and it's illegal."

"Yes," Buster chimed in. "Highly. But only if you get caught."

"Buster, what are you wearing?" Ari lifted one eyebrow.

"What?" Buster ran both hands down his black velvet catsuit. Then kicked out a leg to admire his black leather, knee-high, clunky heel boots. "I told you I have a date and I ain't got time to go back home and change. Take me as I am." He waved his hand in a wide flourish to display his body.

Ari held her lips in a tight smile with a nod. Holding back a laugh as she said, "You're right. Let's go before we get caught."

TALL PINE TREES filled the Woodland Glen cemetery. It looked more like a park than a graveyard, but the headstones and mausoleums destroyed that illusion. A brick wall blocked the world away on three sides and two wrought-iron gates allowed it in. A huge main entrance and a smaller one near the back. During the year, Ari would enter through the gap in the rear fence. Not during this time of year though. The cemetery owners upped security after someone spray-painted the headstones, pulled potted plants from their pots, and broke stained-glass windows during Halloween. Vandalism of this sort has happened for the past few years.

A chain-link fence ran along the oldest part of the cemetery. The car wash next door closed down a few years ago. The oleander shrubs on their side of the fence were once nicely maintained, but now the tall evergreens blocked out the unsightly building along with the fence. Ari had visited often enough during the summer she'd made a small opening in the corner of the greenery.

Ari loosened the chain-link fence and peeked through the oleander branches. Buster closed it behind her, but she thrust out her arm and whispered, "Wait."

A motor whirled in the not too far distance. Then two lights turned on the paved road in front of the row of headstones. Security rolled by on a golf cart. She watched the red tail-lights disappear into the darkness beyond the trees.

"Go." Ari held the branches just wide enough for them to squeeze by. Then clipped the fence back on an extended nail, even though it was hardly noticeable.

First, Nyah, then Buster's hand thrust through with their two bags. "Nyah, hold these," Buster whispered. He climbed through once she took them.

Ari hopped through, replaced the fencing on a top and bottom screw to close the opening, then led their group through the maze of headstones.

"Well, hello," a young girl's voice said. "Whatchus guys up to?"

The light-haired, petite New Yorker died a few months ago, and now she'd become the eyes and ears of the cemetery.

Ari looked down at the small ghost who walked along with the group. "Hey, Krista," she whispered.

Buster looked around and waved.

"He can see me?"

Ari nodded.

"Who are you talking to?" Nyah looked between Ari and Buster.

"But she can't." Krista pointed towards Nyah. After Ari nodded again, Krista rushed to talk to Buster.

"Cemeteries have ghosts, Nyah. But most are friendly," Ari supplied when Buster didn't respond. Krista was talking his ear off.

The young woman nodded, but looked around more warily.

The grounds were extensive and where they needed to go was nearly a mile in towards the center of the property. They entered a stretch of uneven land Ari referred to as Chapel hill, because the buildings all resembled small chapels.

She thrust her arm out and motioned Buster and Nyah to hide next to the wall. Krista stopped as well, but leaned out to see why they'd stopped. A small light illuminated the area on the path they were just on, moving back and forth, up and down, then around a few times. The security guard had ear buds in and was enjoying his music. A bit of dust kicked up as he moved. It loosely resembled the electric slide. Very loosely.

"He's new and he dances all night," Krista said to no one in particular. "Not very good about securing, anything."

Once he cleared the row, the group ran across the path to one of the few mausoleums with steps leading up to eight-foot green granite doors. Carved in large block letters above the entrance read - O'Malley. Buster and Nyah stayed on the side of the large chapel replica. Buster handed Ari her bag before she walked up the stairs to the entrance.

Krista followed her up the steps. She looked up at the name, then back towards Nyah and made a small noise, then whispered as if everyone could hear them. "Eep! Is that her? She was a fashion icon when I followed her on all the social media sites. What happened to her?" Then the little Bronx princess looked at her with wide eyes. "Did you bring her back? I didn't know you could do that?"

Ari was rummaging through her bag, but stopped abruptly. "Because I can't."

Krista lifted a brow and looked at Nyah, then her again. "Really? Cause she's standing right there."

"Fine, she's there. Yes, I brought her back but—"

"I want to see my Pop-Pop."

The hope in the young ghost's eyes broke Ari's heart. Her grandfather, Pauppen Miller was the only family she had left and he didn't visit the cemetery much.

Ari squatted down on her haunches. "Krista, I'm sorry, but I can't do what you want and I can't make him come here. I think it's hard on him to know you're here because he was driving that day."

"It was an accident. It wasn't his fault," Krista said softly, then her lips tightened into a straight line. As she faded away, one small hand wiped at her eyes.

Ari opened her bag and pulled out a small jar of olive-green cream. She dapped a little on her finger, then moved it deftly and quickly left to right, then in a circle over the door. She'd placed a ward after placing Haviland's body inside a few months back, but it let dismages come without harm. The door groaned as she pushed it open.

She looked around, then waved them in. Between the walking security and the cart, they would have to work quickly.

Nyah whispered as she walked in. "The door. What did she do? Was that the runes? I couldn't really see."

Buster nodded. "You know about runes?"

"Only what Ari told me."

Ari heard the gravel grinding under tires and pushed the door closed quickly. "Get down." She motioned as she squatted down. The others dropped where they stood.

A long beam from a flashlight came through the stained-glass window. It lingered long enough that Ari thought they'd been busted. The soft hum of the golf cart idled outside.

"I thought I saw something," a voice came from just outside the door.

Ari looked around. She didn't have time to cast a spell or cause a diversion. She laid against the door, hoping the guy wouldn't play Superman and use all of his strength. His feet shuffled as he came up the stairs. The light moved to just under the door. Ari braced for the push.

"Dude, ain't nobody alive in there. They dead. Come on, I'm hungry," another male voice called out.

The light held steady for a few seconds more before finally disappearing, along with the security guard's footfalls down the steps, onto the rocky gravel. Ari didn't think a golf cart had much get up and go. The spinning tires tossed the rocks around. That guy must have really been hungry.

When she no longer heard anything, Ari quickly pulled items out of her bag. "We don't have much time."

She placed a black candle, and sage smudge stick on the large gold inlaid sarcophagus in the middle of the room. Buster pulled a small silver and gem adorned knife from his bag.

"Nyah, we're going to take a few precautions to ensure you make it back to us."

"What? I thought you did this before." Nyah looked between the two of them.

Ari didn't want to get into the logistics of losing her soul. "We have but this is dangerous on a regular day. Do you still want to do this? We can just pack it up."

"No, I have to." Nyah shook her head fiercely. "I've watched your mating programmings. This is the only way to get—" She looked between Ari and Buster, not finding the right word.

"Closure," Ari supplied.

Nyah nodded, then repeated, "Yes, closure."

"Okay, ladies. We might want to get this party started before those boys swing back around."

Ari nodded and pulled out a large ziplock bag with a dry red substance and poured a line of it at the entrance.

"What's that?" Nyah asked from over her shoulder.

"Crushed brick dust."

"Wow, you pulled out the big guns," Buster said after a low whistle.

"Better safe, than sorry." Ari continued to pour.

Crushed brick dust had been used for centuries as protection around homes and businesses. Keeping away evil spirits or deterring ill-willed people. She'd even read that the dust was used to protect treasures in the ancient pyramids in Egypt.

After lining the windows, Ari returned to the sarcophagus. She ran her fingers over the deep carvings of Gaelic words and rune symbols. The words were actually a spell to aide in the safe travel to the other side.

Ari rummaged through her bag, then patted the top of the ornate coffin. "Lie down."

Nyah tried a few ways but couldn't get on the structure easily. The sarcophagus was wide, but curvy. After struggling, Buster and Ari each grabbed an arm and lifted her up.

After a moment of looking, she pulled out a small jar and opened it.

"Mmm, that smells good. What is it?" Buster placed an unlit candle near Nyah's head.

Ari held it out to him, and he inhaled. "It's rosemary, sage, and anise."

"May I?" Nyah lifted up to inhale. "That smells wonderful."

Buster pulled a glass vial of white salt from his bag and began to pour it around the sarcophagus. Ari dipped her finger into the herb concoction and motioned for Nyah to lay back down. Her finger moved deftly as she created runes depicting the sun, moon, earth, and sea at the head, foot and both sides of Nyah's body. In the same pattern as North, South, East, and West when performing a ritual.

"Buster, check to see if the guards are coming back around. The candle has to stay lit during her entire time in Otherworld. I'd rather not get caught at this point."

Buster clapped his hands together, releasing any stray salt before going towards the small windows. Ari laid dried lavender and chamomile around Nyah's body.

"What's this?"

"A little something to help you find your way home," Ari said with a smile. "How are we—"

"Get down." Buster squatted quickly as a light paused on the windows.

The light held only a moment a two, but it seemed like a lifetime.

Buster peeked through the bottom quarter of the small stained-glass window to verify the security guard had left the area. "Whew, I almost missed him because he was walking. I was listening for the golf cart. But that wasn't the security guard."

Buster moved towards Nyah's head near the candle, just inside the salt and crushed brick circle. Ari stood over her with the Leise's family amethyst in her hand.

"Who was it then?"

"Only one man follows you around," Buster said, with a smirk as he lit the candle.

"Geez, let's just get this done. He's a bad penny if there ever was one."

Ari couldn't understand what it was about her that intrigued Detective Westin so much. He was absolutely sure she was murdering people and anytime anything weird went on in town, he came looking for her.

"Thirty minutes. No more than that or we might actually get caught with your boyfriend prowling the grounds." He pressed buttons on his watch and faintly little beeps echoed through the quiet space.

"Will it hurt?" Nyah asked, eyes flicking between Ari and Buster worriedly.

Buster took her hand in his. "Just relax." He smiled, then she did as well. And when she exhaled, he cut her finger.

"Ouch," Nyah exclaimed as she snatched her hand out of his and rose up like she was ready to bolt.

"Buster!" Ari whispered sharply all why trying to keep Nyah in place. "Sorry, Nyah. We need blood for the spell." She glared at Buster while still talking to Nyah. "He could have told you that before doing it."

Nyah's eyes filled with tears and only fell when she nodded.

"It was faster my way."

"Not helping, Benedict Calaveras," Ari said in a motherly 'you're already in trouble' tone. Plus, she knew saying his real name would shut him up. "Lay back down, it's all painless from this point on. Buster, I need the knife."

"Athame," he corrected.

"The sharp thingie," Ari countered with her hand out and one regal brow arched up.

He nicked his finger, and a small bit of blood mingled with Nyah's before he handed it to Ari.

"Why did he do that?" Nyah's eyes flitted between Ari and Buster.

"It's to ground your spirit to someone on this world."

"Couldn't it have been you?" Nyah lowered her voice, turning away from Buster.

"My spirit energy is nowhere near strong enough to hold you. I know what he did was wrong, but you can trust Buster."

Nyah looked back at him and tightened her lips. She didn't look convinced, but she gave a tight nod.

"Close your eyes." When she did, Ari touched each eye and her head with the amethyst and a little bit of blood. "Calm your heart and mind. I'm going to put you in a sort of half-sleep. I need for you to think about him. The spell should take you straight to him or at least in the general area. And when you're ready to come back, think of home. The smell of the flowers around you here and the candle should help light your way back."

It didn't take long. The candle fluttered.

"Nyah," Ari whispered.

No response. With Nyah's spirit gone, Royal's body held no life and became deathly still. It was disconcerting, actually.

"I guess all we can do is wait," Buster said, still staring at the body.

Ari moved to sit on a concrete bench under one of the stained-glass windows. Not until this moment did she realize something about Nyah's reincarnation creeped her out. She found being around graveyards and ghosts natural. Something about this moment, seeing Royal's dead body, made Nyah's being here seem wrong. This all started by her trying to keep her word to Haviland, but right now, something in her wanted to leave Nyah's spirit just where it was.

"A penny for your thoughts," Buster said, as he sat next to her.

Ari shook away the morbid thoughts. It was just this time of year and this place making her feel this way. "Nothing. It's just when this is over I gotta get this girl out of my house."

CHAPTER 9

Time seemed to come to a standstill as Ari and Buster waited for Nyah to come back to this plane of existence. The crickets chirped, and an owl hooted in the far distance. The lamp post from the path provided enough illumination through the window to keep them from being immersed in total darkness.

Buster finally broke the silence. "Why isn't she staying with him? Wasn't that the entire point of this? You bring her back and he'd give you the spell to release Brennan?"

"Yeah," Ari whispered. "But she said she could hear everything Haviland did in her name."

"And she wasn't pleased?"

Ari nodded.

"Makes sense." Buster nodded as well. "Imagine being trapped, while watching death and destruction rain down all around you, and you can do nothing to stop it. I couldn't see myself with that person either. But what is she going to do? Especially looking the way she does. It's not like she can just walk around and not be noticed."

"Deny, deny, deny, if anyone asks and get her out of Houston. Maybe even Texas." Ari stood over Nyah's body. "She is a slob and goddess knows she can't cook to save her life, but she's a nice person."

Buster stood on the other side of the body, then looked at his watch and nodded.

Ari leaned in and whispered into her ear. "Nyah, it's time." Then pulled a bottle of water from her bag.

"Is that moon or solar infused water?"

"I find the lunar infused water works better on night rituals." Ari cracked open the bottle and poured it into a small wooden bowl.

Ari murmured a prayer before dipping her finger into the water. She touched Nyah's lips. "Enter this realm now, retaining all the knowledge for which you sought." She dabbed the center of her forehead with water. "Look upon this world with thine own eyes and know us as friends." She wiped away the blood from each eye, then touched the amethyst over Nyah's heart. "Return spirit and be at peace."

When Ari blew out the candle, Nyah bolted up out of her dead-like state with a gasp.

Buster wrapped his arms around her and held her. "It's okay. You're back."

Tears welled in Nyah's eyes when she pulled back to look between Ari and Buster. "That place. I would never have imagined." She patted Buster's hand and he released her. She moved slowly and let her feet hang over the edge. "It was so real. I looked like me, felt like me. I was home."

"Do you want to go back? I can put Royal's body back—"

Nyah wiped away tears as she shook her head. "I cannot. Hav did some things—" She bit her bottom lip, staving off the words. After the span of a few heartbeats, she took a deep breath, then continued, "Is his body nearby?"

Ari was taken aback by the sudden change of topic. "Oh, sure. Yes, he's here."

Nyah hopped down. "Could I see him?" She cleared her throat. "One last time."

Ari didn't want to be in the cemetery longer than they had to be now that Detective Douchebag a.k.a. Adam Westin was sniffing around. But she couldn't say no to this final request. "Of course."

Ari quickly rummaged through her bag and pulled out Haviland's spell book.

Nyah gasped. "Where..." her hands reached for the tattered, leather-bound book of their own accord, "...did you get that?"

"Heath, I mean Haviland gave it to me. To help me release you."

Haviland had lied, murdered, and betrayed many people. With Ari, he used a glamour to make himself look younger and called himself, Heath. She'd trusted him up until the point he'd tried to kill her and Leise.

Nyah seemed to come back to her senses and snatched her hand back before touching it, meeting Ari's eyes. "May I?"

Ari nodded, then held it out to her.

"It's just been so long." Nyah ran her fingers over the cover reverently. She held it to her nose and inhaled. The biggest smile spread across her face. "I gave this to Hav many moons ago."

She opened the book not seeming to look for anything in particular. Just touching the pages. "I barely recognize my own hand."

It all became clear to Ari. This was her book; the translations and new spells must have been his additions to the book over the centuries. The book contained spells that consisted of glyphs and runes, that were completely indecipherable. The Gaelic words along the edges of the tome, and even some spells in Latin were Haviland's work, Ari suspected.

Nyah turned the book around. "Did you use this one to hide his body?"

Ari squinted at the small print, then saw her own notes down the side. Haviland recited the spell to her, but she recognized it.

"I can help you. Bring him back. The spell varies a little," Nyah said with a shy smile.

"Even though you remember the spells, Royal didn't have any affinity for magic," Buster said, with some tightness in his voice.

"I never had the gift to begin with," Nyah mumbled. "But I can read it and Ari can repeat it."

"Buster, that would make this go by much faster. Unless you can recite the reveal spell?"

Buster held up his hands in surrender.

"Great." Ari smiled. "Let's do this."

NYAH SAID her goodbyes quickly and they got out of the cemetery just as security was making another pass.

Ari walked backward as she talked. "I think that went well. Once or twice I thought we were gonna get caught."

Buster stopped in his tracks.

"What?" Ari followed his lead. "What's wrong?"

Buster didn't say a word, but he pointed a purple polished fingernail to something behind her.

"Ms. Mason."

She didn't need to turn around to know who was behind her. The disdain dripped from his baritone voice even when he was just saying her name. She took a deep breath before turning around.

"Who's that?" Nyah whispered.

"Trouble," Buster responded in kind. "Ari, you okay?"

Ari nodded. "Yeah, I got this." Then started towards their cars.

"Evening, detective."

He peeled his butt from Tiffany's hood. He had some nerve sitting on her car, but in the interest of getting out of this, she kept her cool… or as much as she could where this man was concerned. She kept her hands to her sides and tried not to fidget too much.

"Out for a midnight stroll?" He stood in front of her with his arms folded.

"Exercise is good for the mind and body." Ari put on a mega-watt smile.

"May I ask where did you stretch your legs tonight?"

"You may ask." Ari kept up the smile.

He nodded. "You want to introduce your friends? Wait, I know you." He pointed at Buster, then he shifted his attention to Nyah.

He looked her over then extended his hand. Ari moved between them.

"It's okay, Ari," Nyah said from behind her.

Ari turned around, squinted, and flitted her eyes towards the policeman and back. Trying to convey that she didn't really need to know this man. Nyah hadn't learned those social cues yet and moved past her with her hand extended.

"I'm Nyah."

"A pleasure, Nyah." He shook her hand but didn't release it readily. "What are you guys doing out so late?"

Nyah smiled. "Breaking up with my mate."

Buster covered his eyes, then his mouth. Ari looked towards the heavens for answers.

"Oh, a break-up." He released her hand, then staggered.

"Detective, are you okay?" Nyah extended her hand to touch him again. She looked around, but neither Ari nor Buster moved to assist them.

He caught himself and shook his head. "Yeah, just stepped on a rock or something."

Nyah nodded, then released him. "And what are you doing out tonight? Working?"

"Just passing by," Detective Westin said with another head shake. "When I recognized Ms. Mason's car. Figured she was up to no good. I almost called it in, since I'm off duty." He tightened his lips quickly and looked around worriedly.

"Really?" Ari moved towards the driver's side of her car. "Good to know. Nyah. Buster. Time to go."

"Right," Buster said, putting a little pep in his step. He opened the door for Nyah before getting into his own car.

Ari stood inside her open door and spoke in a cordial tone although she wanted to scream at the man. "Have a good night, detective."

He frowned but didn't open his mouth. Ari couldn't put her finger on it but she was certain he said more truth than he'd meant to.

Ari knew she would see him again. The man was like a bad penny - he just kept turning up.

CHAPTER 10

A bone-deep chill made Ari do a full-body shiver as she sat straight up in bed. Little puffs of smoke came from her mouth as she spoke. "Did you just float through me?"

"Well, yeah, Cher, how else was I gon' wake you?" Remy stared from her bedside.

Moving each hand up and down her arms to get some warmth back into them. "I don't know, maybe saying something like, 'Cher, you beautiful goddess, please wake up.'" She lowered her voice a couple of octaves to mimic him.

"Really?" Remy guffawed. He actually floated into the air he was laughing so hard. "That would have never worked."

"It's not that funny."

"Oh, Cher but it is." He wiped his cheek and eyes like tears were falling.

"What's got you in such a tissy that you had to wake me up?"

"C'est elle," Remy grumbled.

Ari already knew the 'her' he was referring to. "What did she do now?"

He let out an exacerbated sigh. "She's singing."

He said it like he'd just stepped into a pile of poop. Ari covered her mouth to stop the giggle that bubbled up. "Singing?"

She found it weird that she squinted her eyes now that she tried to listen to the croonings of her visitor. "I don't hear anything," she said, straining to listen. She even got out of bed and cracked open her door to hear. She turned back to him with a raised brow in question.

"What? She was and then she started doing that twirling thing with her arms spread wide." He spun his finger around in a fierce circle. "Like that movie you watch at Christmas." He shivered.

Ari lifted her hand to stifle another giggle, but she couldn't help it. Who knew that singing and dancing could scare a ghost? "Why don't you like her?"

"I don't know, Cher. Something's not right with her. It's like she's dead but not. Like she's living, but not that either. There's a warmth that reverberates from living, breathing humans, even animals. But her… nothing."

Finally, he'd said what was really bugging him. Ari kind of understood what he was referring to. She'd tried to read her but Nyah doesn't have an aura. She thought one would come later, or something mystical would happen with the ancient woman's revival, but nothing.

"Did something happen at the cemetery?" Remy paced.

"Not really. She said her good-byes, then we came home." Ari hunched her shoulders. "Why?"

"I don't know. It feels like she's watching me. Please be careful around her, Aramais," Remy finished.

She'd been blowing off his feelings about Nyah. Thinking it was just good-natured jealousy. It had only been them for many years. But for the first time, he showed true concern, and he never used her given name. "You know she can't see you, but thanks. I'll be careful. But honestly, she's harmless. A little lost perhaps, but she doesn't even have magic."

Remy shook his head disapprovingly.

"Remy, she told me that her life was pretty bad. She had no magic; her legs were frail. She couldn't walk."

No matter what she said Remy never lost the scowl. "Non! I will keep a watch on her."

Something crashed. "Sorry!" Nyah yelled from another room. "I'll clean it up."

Ari knew she couldn't hide in her room any longer. She took a shower and made herself presentable before entering the normal state of her kitchen since Nyah had entered her life.

Chaotic.

Today, only half a loaf of burnt bread filled the trash can, along with what looked like then entire dozen of eggshells, and broken dishes. The once white stove reminded her of a Jackson Pollock original work of art.

Ari opened the door to a nearly empty fridge, but thank goodness, Nyah didn't care for orange juice, one of the few things she left untouched. She poured a glass and grabbed a bottle of water from the inside door. She sipped her juice and took a seat at the wooden farmhouse table. Nyah promptly laid a chipped plate filled with very well-done scrambled eggs and two slices of extra dark brown, nearly burnt toast down in front of her.

Nyah's smile could have lit up the room. She gave a 'tada' wave at the breakfast, then shook out her patchwork maxi dress. "Looks good, yes?"

The hoodie and tennis shoes completed Nyah's look. Ari thought she looked nothing like Royal now. No one should recognize her. *Should* being the operative word. Even with her gorgeous looks, she didn't look exactly like the internet fashionista. More like a hippy cousin.

Ari wasn't sure if the young woman was referring to the dress or the breakfast. She nodded with the glass still to her lips just to be safe. She tapped the corner of the toast on the plate. "Butter?"

Nyah snapped her fingers and jumped up. "I forgot." She brought back the butter and jam. After Ari used them, so did she.

Ari bit into the well-done bread and then wiggled a back tooth to check to make sure she hadn't knocked it loose. After finishing her juice, she cracked open the bottle of water and took a long drink. "I have a few stops I have to make today. Are you up for it?"

"Yes," Nyah said, through a mouth full of eggs. "I've been looking forward to this. Will I meet some more witches?"

Ari thought this a strange question, but she'd only met Buster and had been locked away all this time. She had to be thirsty to meet some new people. "Sure, you'll meet a lot of people." She stood up. "You ready?"

"Are you not going to finish?" Nyah pointed with her fork towards the untouched eggs.

Ari blinked, then looked at the untouched breakfast. "You know, I'm not really hungry this morning." She patted her stomach before walking away.

A growl rattled against her ribs. Oh, yeah, it was going to be a long day.

CHAPTER 11

"We won't be here long." Ari said, as she and Nyah walked up the covered walkway.

The bloodstain on the senior facility entrance was all but gone. They must have power-washed it out with bleach. A few months back one of the employees was killed by an evil witch. That murderer happened to be Nyah's husband, Haviland.

Goosebumps rolled up Ari's arm as a cool chill flowed over her, then she caught the scent. It was there and gone so fast, but she was positive she caught a whiff of Sandalwood, with a bit of moss and orange blossoms.

Chantilly perfume.

Ravenswood Arms always smelled like Nurse Frankie. This was the first time Ari had smelled it since the older woman's passing. She took a few deep breaths and looked around. She didn't see Frankie's spirit, but she could feel it and that was enough.

She wasn't sure why the woman had come back. Maybe to protect her old stomping grounds. Maybe to protect the people in it. Maybe she just wasn't ready to cross over. She could never presume to know what a spirit was thinking. They were unpredictable on the best of days. She should know, she'd lived with one most of her life.

Ari slowed down when she saw Krista's grandfather walking in her direction. When he got closer, Ari lifted her hand to wave. "Hello, Mr. Miller."

The silver-haired gentleman looked her dead in the eyes and walked past her. The older man couldn't move fast, so it was plainly obvious that she was being snubbed. Sometimes Ari could be aggressive to get what she wanted. Getting him to the cemetery only worked once and he had refused to talk to her or go visit Krista's grave since.

Nyah leaned over and whispered in Ari's ear. "I don't think he like you."

That was an understatement. "I know. He has his reasons."

"Ari," a happy voice called out.

Ari and Nyah turned to see a tall woman in a nice pantsuit walking towards them.

"What are you doing out here?" Lane Exley said, with a big smile.

"Hi, Lane. We were just about to come in. I brought help today. This is Nyah."

Lane extended her hand towards Nyah. "Well, hi. I'm Lane. The facilities director."

Nyah looked at Ari first before taking the woman's hand. "Nice to meet you."

Lane studied Nyah's face for a long moment. "You remind me of someone."

Nyah turned quickly to look around at nothing particular, just breaking eye contact.

"Anyway, let's get you guys signed in." They walked through the glass front doors. "Ari, my skin is parched did you bring me..."

Ari held out the brown paper bag before she could finish.

"Oh, my goodness, you are a life saver. This stuff is like miracle cream, clears away blotches in hours instead of days. It's like..."

"Magic," Ari interjected with a smile and waving her fingers in a woogie fashion.

Ari and Lane laughed but Nyah looked at them with a blank face. Ari knew she didn't get the joke.

Instead of the clipboard at the check-in desk, Lane walked them to the back office. "We have a new system." She stopped in front of a new slim monitor and keyboard. "Volunteers sign-in here now. Here is your badge." She handed one with a picture to Ari. "And a guest badge for you. Ari called ahead so I got this one ready, but if you like it here and want to come regularly, we'll do some paperwork. No problem. But for today this will work fine."

Nyah gently took the rigid plastic card in two hands and gave a small bow. "Thank you."

Lane let out an uncomfortable laugh. "Okay. So, just type your name, then wave the barcode on the back of your badge in front of the camera."

Ari did it first. "All fancy with the new camera."

"It still has its kinks. The camera is motion activated, so we get pictures of people walking by, empty spaces, but most of the time it's just a blur."

Lane's cellphone let out a double beep. "Excuse me, I have to take this. You know where everybody is, except Aracely. She's taken to being in her room lately." She waved good-bye, as she spoke into her phone.

Ari had showed Nyah how to use a computer, and she took to it faster than cooking. Ari waved towards the computer and Nyah tentatively touched the mouse, moved it around, then clicked. A smile lit up her face when she waved her badge and the computer acknowledged her. There was a level of joy Ari hadn't seen in the young woman before and she liked it.

First stop, the game room. Ari could hear Luscious trash talking before she entered the room.

"Gentlemen," a woman in pink scrubs said as she rushed in. "We can hear you all the way down the hall."

"Elena, you can't stop the beatdown train," Luscious said, twirling a domino in the air.

Ari and Nyah walked up next to Elena and Luscious. Michael contemplated the dominoes on the table, then gently laid his piece down.

Luscious slammed down the domino he was holding aloft. "Walk chicken, too fat to fly!" He slammed the domino on the table and the entire table shook.

"Mr. Lafayette," Elena growled. "Please."

"I think it's over," Ari said to no one in particular.

"How do you know?" Nyah whispered.

"That was his last domino."

Elena shook her head and walked out.

"Better luck next time, Rookie," Luscious said, as he placed the dominoes in the box. "Ari, when did you get here?" His hands stopped moving. "Oh, and who's the pretty lady?"

"Boys. Luscious, Michael, this is Nyah. She's thinking about volunteering. Be nice."

The chair scrapped on the hardwood floor as Luscious rose. He took Nyah's hand in his own. "A pleasure." He softly pressed his lips to the back of her hand.

Luscious had been a player since back in the day and being an elder statesman wasn't going to change him.

"Stop mauling her, man. She don't need no old fogey like you slobbering on her," Michael said from the table.

"Shut up, man."

Nyah smiled as she slid her hand from the older man and extended it towards Michael. "Nice to meet you."

Michael clasped it. "Same. I hope you like it here. Some of us can be rowdy, but we're a nice bunch."

"Good to know," Nyah said with a smile.

"Here." Ari held out two paper bags with their names on it.

"Oh, yeah." Luscious said as he looked through the bag. He spoke without looking up. "You make me that cream?"

"I told you I wasn't making that again."

"The blue pill alternative made me a Clydesdale among Shetland ponies." Luscious' chest puffed up a little.

"It made him unbearable, is what it did," Michael said. "Sit down, before you fall down, fool," he said to Luscious.

"The ladies liked it." Luscious moved to sit, and his knee made a grinding noise. Ari grabbed his arm and helped him to his seat.

"I got you both something for your joints," Ari looked at Luscious pointedly. "And some other good stuff."

Luscious groaned.

"Have I ever let you down?"

Luscious let out a breath. "Not until this moment."

Michael lifted the bag. "Thank you. I've been better since you started giving us these teas."

"You're welcome. Now, what's this I hear about Aracely staying in her room?" Ari looked between both of the older men.

Michael finally spoke. "We're not really sure, but I think something is going on with her kids."

Ari nodded. Aracely was a strong woman, but family could break anyone's spirit. "I'll check on her. You boys be good."

When they were far enough away, waiting at the elevators, Nyah turned to her. "Why do you call them boys, when they are clearly elders?"

"It's fun for them. And in most cases, no matter how old a man gets, he still acts like a child."

"This world is different in many ways."

CHAPTER 12

The residential halls were always pretty quiet. Ari and Nyah walked down the spacious carpeted hallway. It was lined with framed abstract artwork, a seating area, fire extinguishers on each end, along with a red wall phone and defibrillator.

"What is this area called? It is like where you live." Nyah touched the wall. "Except for this stuff."

Ari looked at the floral and scroll pattern and was thankful her walls were painted a soft white. "That's called wallpaper, and this is where the residents live." She stopped in front of one door. "Ah, here it is. Look, I'll talk to her. Hopefully, I can get her to go downstairs, maybe even outside."

"Do you want me to leave?"

"No, just hang out on this floor." Ari waved in the general area.

Nyah smiled and nodded before she walked away. Ari knocked on the door.

"Aracely, I know you're in there," Ari said when there was no response.

She waited, but after another minute, maybe two, she knocked and called out again, "Aracely!"

Through the door, Ari could hear a litany of Spanish, before she heard, "Hold your horses!"

The door opened to a frowning older woman. "Ain't you got something better to do?"

"More than seeing you? Nope."

Aracely folded her arms and didn't move her wheelchair from blocking the entrance.

"Com' on Aracely. Do you really think I'd come here and not visit you?" Ari folded her arms, mirroring the older woman. "Well?"

The facade broke. Aracely rolled the chair backward, leaving space for Ari to come into the apartment.

It took only ten minutes before Ari wheeled the older, once cranky woman out of the room.

Aracely giggled as she scolded Ari. "Will you slow down, Mija. I'm an old lady."

"Old lady, my foot. You're one of the strongest women I know." Ari turned the wheelchair around in a circle. "Nyah, where are you?"

Ari looked both ways down the hall.

"Who's Nyah? A friend of yours?" Aracely watched Ari march back and forth a few times.

"I told her to wait," Ari said. "Not really a friend. Just a person I'm helping out. She wanted to see what I did, so I brought her with me today."

"Maybe she got bored and went downstairs. It is nice outside." Aracely pushed the down button on the elevator panel.

Ari thought on it a moment longer, then snapped out of it when the elevator bell dinged. She had mentioned she wanted to take Aracely outside since she had been cooped up in that room. But it was strange that Nyah would wander off like that.

Ari pushed Aracely out of the elevator. "Why don't you ever use your electric chair?"

Once on the main floor, Aracely popped Ari's fingers. "I can drive myself. And where am I going that I need to move that fast?" She rolled away slowly. "Besides, this keeps my arms strong."

Ari followed her out the side door to the paved garden path. It meandered through rosebushes, Japanese boxwoods, and the ever heat resistant crepe myrtle. Aracely pulled into the first covered seating area.

"Is that your friend?"

Ari looked up to find Nyah laying in the grass, with no shoes on. Her arms and legs opened, then closed. Then she repeated the motion. If there had been snow on the ground, Nyah would have made a perfect snow angel. She watched the girl, and she had a huge smile on her face the entire time. She finally raised up and smiled even wider when she saw Ari.

"This is glorious." Nyah leaned down and inhaled.

"Your friend is a strange one," Aracely said, still watching the girl.

"Yeah, she's not from around here," Ari said, watching Nyah as she came towards them.

"I like this place." Nyah's eyes glistened. "So many nice people."

Ari thought Nyah was about to tear up and cry, but then she was rolling around in the grass. Royal could be highly allergic for all they knew.

"Why did you run off?"

Nyah seemed non-plussed by the question. "I thought you wanted privacy and time to talk. And you said you were to go outside at some point. I just waited."

"Well, this is my friend, Aracely."

Nyah gave a half bow, then extended her hand, but snatched it back quickly towards her face.

"You okay?" Ari rummaged through her bag and pulled a tissue.

Nyah didn't answer but reared back, Ari put the tissue in her hand as she let out a hellacious sneeze.

Aracely reached into her pocket, pulled out some hand sanitizer and held it open. Nyah looked at Ari. Ari reached both hands out under the open small plastic container. Aracely squeezed a small amount of clear gel into her hands and she put hands together like she was washing them. Nyah mirrored the hand motions. Aracely even sanitized her hands as well.

Nyah didn't hesitate this time, she extended her hand towards

Aracely with a gleaming smile. "Thank you and it's a pleasure to meet you."

Aracely smiled as well and slid her hand into Nyah's. For a moment, Ari felt like a proud momma. Then everything seemed to slow down. Aracely's mouth fell open as if to scream, but no sound came out. She snatched her hand from Nyah's and gripped more under her arm than over her heart. Her breathing became labored, then Ari heard quick intakes. The older woman was having some sort of episode.

She moved directly into her line of sight. "Aracely? Can you hear me?" Aracely gave a nearly imperceptible head movement, but her eyes followed Ari. "Can you speak? What's wrong? Let's get you some help." Ari grabbed the handles and hurried back into the main building.

Nyah followed fast on her heels. "What's wrong?"

"I don't know. Could be a stroke or heart attack." They burst through the automatic doors. "We need some help right here!"

Lane and a couple of nurses rushed towards them, they spoke to her in hushed tones, then a nurse attached a portable oxygen tank, before rolling her away.

"What happened?" Lane asked.

"I don't know. One minute she was fine, the next she clutched her chest." Ari watched as the group of nurses disappeared towards the clinic. "She's going to be okay, right?"

Lane patted her on the shoulder. "Mrs. Hernandez was responsive, and she's strong. I'm sure she'll be up and around in no time."

Ari couldn't help but think this was all her fault. "Do you?" She looked at her feet, then back towards the clinic, before speaking again, "Do you think this is my fault?"

Lane's head moved back and forth before she even finished asking. "Get that out of your head. You probably saved her. She doesn't like to wear her medical alert necklace, and she was in her room alone. Think about that." Lane squeezed her hand before walking away.

Nyah's cold hand touched her shoulder. "Maybe we should go."

Ari wasn't sure how long she'd stood there, but the touch

brought her back. She blinked away tears and nodded before walking towards the exit. The entire incident replayed through her mind and she had to make it up to her friend. She needed to go the White Cauldron anyway, maybe there was something in one of those books to help Aracely. She would get the details from Lane later, then she would whip up something to prevent or send warning bells out the next time something like this happened.

What good is there having power and not being able to help your friends?

CHAPTER 13

The ride to the White Cauldron was a quiet one. Thoughts and spells were racing through Ari's mind, but she wasn't so preoccupied that she hadn't heard Nyah's reactions to the buildings in the city. In the few outings she'd taken Nyah on, they were always at night. She'd finally gotten to experience and see the city, and that eased some of the anxiety. Bringing Nyah to this world was one of the few things that had gone right as of late.

Ari held the door for Nyah. The moment she stepped inside, she knew she hadn't paid attention to the vehicles outside enough. The scent of his cologne greeted her long before she saw him. Just what she needed, a nice chat with her favorite civil servant.

Voices could be heard from the back of the store. Ari turned her back and looked at the new inventory of items on the round table in the entryway. She peeked over at Detective Westin and Elizabeth in the library area.

"Officer, I—"

"Detective," Westin cut in.

"Come again?" Elizabeth questioned.

"It's detective, you said, 'officer.'" He tacked on a seemingly forced, dry chuckle at the end.

"Oh my, I do apologize, Detective Westin. This is all so distressing. I don't know why anyone would say there was a dead body here. I assure you I never saw any blood on the building. Inside or out."

The detective flipped out a card and held it out to her. "If anything weird or suspicious happens. Don't hesitate to call."

Elizabeth took the card gently with a smile. "I most assuredly will. You have a nice day now."

Sugar sweet sarcasm dripped from every last word. Ari had to keep taking breaths to avoid laughing aloud.

"Ms. Mason."

Ari slammed the book shut she was not really thumbing through and met his aquamarine blue eyes. "Detective Westin." All hints of laughter were gone.

He walked past her then turned back. "You wouldn't know anything about the rash of comatose people filling up the hospitals."

"How could I possibly?" A bit of anger bubbled around her words.

"You or someone you know always seem to be around when strange things happen in this town."

Ari lifted a finger as if to make a point, but before she said a word, Nyah slid between them.

"Detective Adam Westin." Nyah extended her hand. "It is good to see you again. Do you remember me?"

Ari watched the scowl melt away and his eyes widen with something that resembled joy. He was happy to see her? He'd only met her once.

He took her hand, then turned it over, to kiss it. "How could I forget? Nyah, such a pleasure to see you again."

Were those dimples? Goddess above, look at those teeth. Adam Westin must have worn braces for forever to have teeth that straight. Ari couldn't believe her eyes. She was in the Twilight Zone right now, that's the only thing that could explain what she was seeing.

Nyah's cheeks turned a bright shade of pink. "Ari tells me you work with death. I hope nothing so unpleasant has happened here."

"False alarm. You're safe here," Westin said.

"Thank you," Nyah said. "Please continue to do the good work."

He gave her a stiff nod, then walked out.

Someone needed to pinch Ari. "What just happened here?" She looked around bewildered. "'False alarm'? 'You're safe here'? He never said stuff like that. And I didn't get a parting jab. That's practically unheard of."

"Do you like him, Ari?" Nyah whispered. "I can call him back."

"What?!" Ari screeched. "Gods, no. I'm just used to him being a certain kind of way." She waved at the door. "Not that. What did you do to him?"

"Me? Nothing." She looked down at her hands. "Maybe it's this body. You said, she had lots of followers. People like her, yes?"

"True. About two million, before… well, before."

"Ladies, so sorry about that," Elizabeth said, as she waved towards the door. "Ari, if I could have a word, please."

Ari gave Elizabeth a nod. She'd wanted to introduce the shop owner to Nyah, but judging by the tightness in her voice and wringing hands, she had something serious on her mind. "Nyah, I'll be right back."

Ari followed Elizabeth to the very back of the library. "What's going on?"

"This." Elizabeth opened a glass jar and grabbed a handful of salt from the bookshelf, then opened the back door and scattered the tiny crystals in the alleyway near the door. "Commostro et revelare."

A pulse of heat emanated from an empty spot just outside the door. The air moved in ripples of waves above a slowly forming body. The crumpled man looked like an island surrounded by a lake of blood. He wore a bright green and orange vest, blue dickies, and work boots. There hadn't been construction in this part of town for at least three months. Where had he come from?

"Who is that?" This was why Westin was snooping around.

"I normally don't pay any attention to things hitting the building. But the blood. There was so much of it." Elizabeth's hand flew to her mouth. "I knew something was wrong because the lights started to flicker on and off, books flew off the shelf. You have to understand. The building rarely does things like that."

Ari walked around the body. With her hand outstretched and eyes closed, she extended her power to try to sense any magic on the body. She didn't feel anything, but her nose twitched. The sickly-sweet aroma had hints of belladonna, arsenic, and something else she'd smelled before. Could be something she had in her own garden?

"Someone poisoned this man. I can't really sense anything else." There had been too much magic used inside and around the building for her to pinpoint one source. "Detective Westin was here looking for him?"

"I'm pretty sure he was. I had only discovered it moments before he arrived."

Why would anyone try to set up the owner of the White Cauldron? Not just owner, what if the person was looking to expose witches? "Have you had any problems with customers? Any witches?"

Elizabeth shook her head. "What are we going to do with him? I can't leave him invisible indefinitely."

"I'll find a place. No man deserves what they did to him." Ari stepped back inside.

Elizabeth whispered a few words as she touched the outside brick wall and the body disappeared and the alley looked as it always did, dirty with discarded paper, and dead leaves.

Once inside, they found Nyah ensconced in a corner reading.

"Good book?" Ari said from over her shoulder.

Nyah wiped away tears. "Sorry. It's just I haven't seen script from my land in a very long time." She closed the book and held it close to her heart.

Ari saw the page before she closed it, there weren't any words, just glyphs and runes.

Elizabeth extended her hands. "May I?"

"Oh, of course." Nyah handed it to the woman.

Elizabeth gently turned the pages. Ari looked over her shoulder. The pages had a tea stain tinge with small pictures in the top corners. They looked more like photographs than hand-drawn art. And the runes were more curved and flared. Some were so closely written together, they resembled an archaic version of calligraphy.

"This is one of this store's oldest tomes. No one has ever been able to read it. But I could never part with it. Until now." Elizabeth handed the book back to Nyah.

Well, that just set the waterworks off. Nyah wiped away tears. "Thank you…" she paused. She must have just realized she didn't know the woman's name.

"Oh, I'm sorry. Nyah, this is Elizabeth. She's the owner of this establishment," Ari chimed in.

"Thank you, Elizabeth."

"You are most welcome. Now, did you ladies come in for something in particular?" Elizabeth clapped her hands together. "How's your new amulet handling the ghosts?"

"Surprisingly, they haven't been around. Weird, I'm normally bombarded by them the closer we get to All Hallows Eve, but this year nothing. Not that I'm complaining." She rapped two knocks on the side of the wooden bookshelf.

"I will sit over there," Nyah said before she went back to her corner.

Ari never thought about how lonely and scary this would be for Nyah. She gave up her lifelong love because he was evil. Now, she's on her own, learning about a new world.

Ari and Elizabeth walked to the front of the store. "I want to see what you have on anxieties and heart conditions."

Elizabeth went to the front bookcase. It held all the new and modern homeopathic treatments. "Heart as in love or attack?"

Ari quickly said, "Attack."

The store owner's floor-length, A-line skirt fluttered as she glided to the next bookcase. Ari imagined paddling feet battling gravity to keep the petite woman afloat and fluid.

"This should help." Elizabeth looked behind her, then lowered her voice. "How's she doing?" She glanced over towards Nyah.

"Pretty good. I mean, for being brought back to life in a world where you don't know a soul. Then, cutting loose ya man after realizing he was a murderous bastard. As well as can be expected."

"No anger issues?"

"No, none. Well, not that I've seen. She's decided," she lifted her hands for air quotes, "'to change the world and help people'. That's why I brought her out. To see if there's anything she wants to start doing."

"Magic?"

"She doesn't have any?" Ari hunched a shoulder.

Elizabeth looked at Ari thoughtfully, then looked back at Nyah. "Maybe you're right." She returned to Ari. "You should bring her to the witch training. The girls would love it. She looks exactly like—"

"Don't say it," Ari grumbled. "I think with the haircut and all, she looks like her own person."

Elizabeth tightened her lips to hold back her smile.

"Seriously?" Ari stared at her friend incredulously. "I think we are going to have to agree to disagree. Heck, how do you even know who Royal is, anyway?"

"I was only born in the nineteenth century. I do own a computer and television, you know."

Info like that still blew Ari's mind.

CHAPTER 14

Between girl-talk with Elizabeth and searching for new spells, time just slipped away from Ari. She rushed through the back door of the Cave.

"Hey, Jacque," Ari said, as she jammed her bag and jacket into her locker.

"Hi, Ms... Ms. Ari," Jacque stammered.

She closed the locker door, then turned to eye him. "What did I say about calling me Miss?"

"To... to not to." Jacque looked down at his feet.

Ari placed a finger under his chin and lifted his head. He averted his eyes. "Jacque, look at me." When he did, she continued, "We're friends, right?"

He nodded, and she smiled. "Well, stop making me feel like an old bar-keep."

"You are an old bar-keep." Bull's voice boomed through the employee break/locker room. "You two quit playing hide the pickle and get out here."

"Bull, you could ruin a wet dream. We were having a moment."

Jacque motioned to move, but she held him in place. Both hands on both cheeks.

"Hey, no touching at work. You might have whatever's going 'round." Bull motioned his hands in a wide gap. "What you two need to do, is get to work."

"I don't have anything, you have anything, Jacque?"

He shook his head back and forth. "No… no, ma'am."

She squinted her eyes at him.

"Sorry." Jacque looked down meekly.

Ari lifted his head and looked him in the eyes and smiled. "We're good."

"Hey," Bull yelled. "Wash your hands before coming back in. The news said they don't know how this thing is spreading."

"Yes, Dad. Now, give us a minute." She rolled her eyes away from Bull, then looked down at the young man she held in her hands. "Real friends don't make young, vibrant women feel old. Do you think I'm old?"

"No." He looked her square in the eyes without a flinch or flutter. "I think you're kind of perfect."

"Oh, you're so sweet." She kissed him on both cheeks. When his face blossomed into a bright scarlet red, she wanted to kiss him again. But he might have a full-on nose bleed if she did that.

"Let's have a good night out there," Ari said before she walked away.

It wasn't chaotic or anything, just a regular night at the bar. Bull made it seem like the place had been overrun with newly turned vampires in need of something to drink. As she worked through the throngs of thirsty patrons, she felt someone watching her. No, it wasn't magic. Just good ol' female intuition. That tingling sensation you feel as hairs rise on the nape of your neck.

Only when a couple of ram-horned, corseted guys moved did she see the reason for her discomfort.

Detective Adam Westin.

Goddess, didn't he have something better to do with his evenings? She made a B-line towards him.

"Don't you have someone else to harass?" Ari said without a hint of a smile.

"Not harassing, just having a drink." Westin lifted his long neck beer.

"Here? You couldn't go anywhere else?" Ari could hear the, 'heys and can you take my orders' as people called out, but she didn't budge from the man in front of her.

He took a long pull from his beer before speaking to her. If he were something more than a dismage, his steely stare would have unnerved her. But as it was, there was no power behind the gaze, just curiosity. Questions that she couldn't answer.

"Ms. Mason, you are an interesting woman. But you are also, sneaky, devious, and full of secrets."

How many beers had he had? He's doing a little too much talking, and he's not even growling at her.

"I am a detective. I will find out what you are hiding. You and your little club."

"Ari!" Bull called from behind her.

She whipped a finger up to stave off anymore yells from her boss, but focused completely on the man before her. "We are just trying to live our best lives. Why can't you understand that?"

"Because death, destruction, and overall weird shit, happens around you. I don't like that."

"I'm not breaking any laws, so you need to back up."

"But when you do. I'll be there." Westin turned up the bottle and finished his beer, then stuffed a few dollars into the tip jar before pushing off his stool and walking away.

"That man. Aargh!" Ari grumbled to herself before getting back to work. She hated that she was on his radar. Even worse, there was nothing she could do to get him off her back.

It had been hours since Detective Westin had parted from the bar, but she still had that feeling like someone was watching her. At this point, it was more annoyance than anything. The bar had slowed down considerably and one bartender could manage it.

"Hey, Bull. I'm gonna take five."

Bull looked around the room then back at her. "You might as well take ten. I can handle this."

Ari slid through the side opening of the bar, but instead of going to the break room or even out back. She walked around the dance floor, near the stage, then between the table and chairs.

That's when she noticed him, in the back corner, looking directly at her.

Leif.

What was he doing here? She hadn't seen him in a few days, thought maybe the attraction she felt was one-sided. But her mother had sent her aunt the first time, this could be her second attempt to get her to come back to the coven. It wouldn't be beneath her.

Ari's breathing sped up as she walked towards him. She tried to still her nerves for whatever he might say.

"What are you doing here?" She slid into the seat across from him.

He tapped the rim of his glass. "Thirsty."

"And?"

He stared at her with those eyes that seemed to see straight through to her soul, but he didn't utter another word. He was *that* guy right now. The Ice-Man.

"You just so happened to be in the neighborhood?"

He took a sip of his drink. It could have been a vodka on the rocks, or gin, she couldn't tell. *Oh, to be the girl that kissed those moist lips.* Ari had to look away. Without doing anything, this man tempted her like no other. He still didn't answer, even after he finished his drink.

As much as she wanted him, she needed to know the truth and prayed he would tell it to her. She stared at his side profile and knew this man could hurt her.

Break her.

"Leif, look I've had a long night and I don't have enough strength to play this game with you." The chair scraped the wood floor as she moved to get up.

His cool hand covered hers. "Wait."

Their eyes connected and the coldness was still there, but not the indifference. He didn't remove his hand, and she didn't make him as she sat back down. They sat in silence for what seemed like an eternity.

"This place." He looked around, tapping the rim of his glass with his other hand. "You've worked here long?"

He did not just start with small talk, but she answered anyway. "A while. Is that what you really want to say? Because my break is nearly over."

He stopped tapping his glass. "I want to get to know you."

"Did your high priestess send you to 'get to know me?'"

"No. I came on my own."

"You know it's against coven law to interact with me in any way, right?" Ari tried to pull her hand from his, but he held firm.

"I am aware."

"You can't. My mother..."

“Isn't here.” He leaned in, keeping his eyes on hers. “This is about you and me.”

And right then, fear slithered up her spine and settled. He was serious about them. She looked at her watch. "Um, I have to get back to work." She pointed behind her. Fumbling as she slid out of his grip, backed out of the chair, then knocking it to the floor. All her coordination flew out the window along with her wits.

"We'll talk. Soonish. Yeah, gotta go." English didn't seem to be her first language all of the sudden.

Through the mix of people talking, and loud music, she could have sworn she heard him say, "I'll wait for you."

She wasn't sure if that was for tonight or forever. Her brain wasn't good for much at this point and that was all right. A girl could dream though. Right?

CHAPTER 15

Jacque and Bull had taken to walking Ari to her car after work every night. Even though the back parking lot was about as big as a Kleenex. Just as they stepped out of the door, a cool breeze sent goosebumps over Ari's arms.

"Hey," Ari said. The words were barely out of her mouth when Jacque whisked her behind him. She didn't know he could move like that.

Leif said nothing as he came out of the shadows.

"Bull, don't!" Ari saw Bull's hand move towards his piece in the small of his back. He was more of the 'ask questions later' kind of guy.

"Sonofabitch, man, I could have shot you," Bull growled. He slowly brought his hand out from behind him, without a gun. "It's freaking Texas. Shoot first, just keep that in mind for next time, Loverboy. I might have to hang the sign on the door if your men keep showing up back here."

"It hasn't been that many," Ari said sheepishly.

He gave her the, 'you know better' look, before saying, "Looks like you are well-protected. I'm out." Bull threw a hand up and walked away. The motorcycle roared to life, then her boss kicked up gravel as he burned out of the parking lot.

Ari touched Jacque's shoulder as she slid around him. "Jacque, it's okay. He's my…" What was he to her? They weren't lovers. At least, not yet. *Whoa, girl. Keep your panties on.* "This is Leif. A family friend."

Both men stared at each other, but neither extended a hand. More like they sized each other up. Leif squinted and tilted his head back and forth, regarding the smaller man.

"What are you?" Leif whispered.

"This is Jacque, my co-worker," Ari said, as she looked between the men. Her head moved back and forth like a ping-pong ball. The tension was thick, a machete might not even slice through it.

"Okay."

Ari didn't have time for male posturing. Goddess save her from protective men. Before she reached her blue BMW, a dreadlocked and tattered man lunged out at her. A familiar warmth flared through her body as she stumbled backward. Heavy footfalls pounded behind her. Before she could get a blast off, a strong arm wrapped around her waist and pulled her against him. Jacque stood between her and the homeless man, with his hand out.

The man crumpled to the ground as he let out a gut-wrenching scream.

"What is he?" Leif said in a reverent whisper.

Ari never felt anything different about Jacque, but magic didn't work inside the bar either. That was sort of the reason she picked the location. For a few hours, a couple of days a week, she didn't worry about anyone or think about magic or any of the trappings that came with it. Now, she had to wonder if that was a mistake.

Through the man's grunts and screams, Ari made out one word. Her name.

She broke from Leif's hold, but she didn't dare touch Jacque. "Stop it! Whatever you're doing stop it."

Jacque didn't stop. Ari moved in front of him and excruciating pain lanced her. She couldn't even think enough to speak. Nothing coherent would have come out of her mouth anyway. It was only a moment, but it felt like a lifetime.

"Ari, what the hell do you think you're doing?" Jacque lowered his hand.

What was that? It was like he sucked the life right out of her. Ari swayed on her feet. Two sets of hands reached for her and she snatched away from them. "I'm okay. Just give me a minute."

When she was sure she wouldn't fall down, she squatted next to the man she believed to be her cousin. Moving the dreadlocks from his face, she placed her finger under his nose. A slight puff of wind caressed it. He wasn't dead.

"Lucas? Is that you?"

"Forgotten about me so soon?" His voice held a mere fraction of the rich, deep sound she was accustomed to.

She all but fell down and pulled him into her lap. She nearly tossed him, he was so light. It was like lifting a child. Tears streamed down her face. "Where have you been? I've been looking for you for months."

He tried to speak, but it sounded like he was about to hack up a lung. She couldn't remember the last time she really hated someone, but she summoned all the venom in her heart and focused it on Jacque.

"What did you do to him?"

"I… I," Jacque stammered as he looked around bewildered. "I thought he was going to hurt you. Please, Ms. Ari, don't… don't hate me."

He took a step towards her and she held up a finger to stop him. "Okay. Just stop." She couldn't get into it with him. Her cousin laid half-dead or at least lingering somewhere between life and death in her arms. "But we will have a long talk about this." She waved her finger around the man in her arms.

Jacque nodded vigorously and stepped back further, but didn't leave.

Her cousin closed his eyes. For a moment her heart stopped. "Lucas?" She projected a level of calm into her voice that she didn't actually possess. "What do you need?"

"Thirsty."

Ari looked up, but before she could ask, Jacque had already started back towards the bar. She touched her cousin's face, and the mud flaked off in her hand.

Jacque returned but stopped short. Lucas opened his eyes at the same time. Pea gravel went everywhere as he dug in his heels trying to getaway.

"Calm down." Ari held her hand up to stop Jacque, then pointed towards Leif. "He's not going to hurt you," Ari said, over and over as she held him steady.

Jacque handed the bottle of water to Leif. The tall man squatted down and cracked open the bottle. Ari took it from him and pressed it to Lucas' lips. His eyes were glued to the dark figure on the edge of the parking lot.

"Don't worry about him." She turned his head towards the bottle. "Just drink." She helped him hold the container. Water went everywhere except in his mouth.

Leif looked behind him, then moved to block the view of the man. Ari gave him an appreciative nod. "Can you hold him for a moment?"

Leif frowned but nodded. "Lucas, I'll be right back. This is my friend, Leif. You know him, right?"

Lucas tore his mouth away from the bottle. "Aramais, don't go near him."

"Trust me. I'll be okay." Ari walked towards the edge of the parking lot.

Jacque paced back and forth but stopped when Ari arrived. "Is he okay?"

Ari looked back at her cousin, then back to him. "I think he'll be alright."

"I didn't mean to hurt him. Please believe me."

Jacque reached for her and Ari stepped back. She could see the hurt in his eyes, but she wasn't sure what his power was or how it worked.

"I'm sorry," Jacque said, placing his hands behind his back.

"Jacque, I do believe you. But what you did…" Ari shook her head. "What are you?"

"I'm afraid when I tell you, we won't be friends anymore." He kicked the gravel around.

Ari was a little afraid of him, but he was also her friend. "Jacque Delacroix, I am now and will always be your friend. No matter what you are. Now, you can control those, right?" She pointed towards his hands. "It's not just inside the bar that they don't work?"

He looked at his hands, then nodded.

She opened her arms. "I'm trusting you. You trust me?"

He was sobbing before he wrapped his arms around her. He nearly knocked her over with the force of his hug. "Thank you."

Something special had just happened, but Ari wasn't sure exactly what yet. They agreed to meet for coffee, and he would tell her everything.

She walked back to the other two men, Lucas watched her with something close to panic in his eyes. "Are you okay?"

"Yeah, I'm fine. You?"

He nodded. "I've been better, but they still have Luca Bee."

Luca Bee was Lucas' twin sister. He was the only one who still called her that; she went by Rumble or Rum because of her earth magic.

"Who has her?" This time Ari couldn't keep the alarm out of her voice. *A rival coven? An ex-boyfriend?* Although Rum should be able to handle anyone by dropping them in a deep pit and covering them up to their necks in dirt.

"The coven."

Ari wasn't sure she'd heard him right. "Excuse me. Who's coven? Our… your coven?"

He nodded, then lifted the bottle for another drink.

"Leif, what's going on at the coven?"

"I'm not in the know, Princess," Leif said.

As Ari sat on the ground, she gave him the evil eye. No need to get into the 'I'm not a Princess' squabble again.

"Your mother wants more power." Lucas finally moved out of

Ari's arms and sat up on his own. "After the rumors about a witch who could steal magic were confirmed, she became obsessed."

"And she found out about Haviland and that you guys helped me." It was a statement, not a question. "Is that why she did this? She wants him?"

"Him, his secrets, his grimoire, everything."

"What did you tell her?"

Lucas' eyes lowered. "There wasn't much to tell her. He was powerful, we fought, and you imprisoned him."

"But why do this? I don't understand."

"I didn't say anything at first, denied it all, then they found out about Rum helping your tween witches and figured she must have been there for the big fight."

"This is over the line, even for my mother."

"I think this was punishment."

"For what?"

"Choosing you over her," Lucas sighed.

"That wasn't what happened at all."

"We know that. And now she really wants you married into the Louisiana coven," Lucas said, sounding more like himself.

"Why? What does my mother get out of it?" *Besides controlling me.*

"Before my untimely incarceration, I'd overheard mother say that coven had beaucoup money, but were cursed."

"What kind of curse?" Leif reached for the empty bottle. Lucas hunched his shoulders. "Our coven tortured you? You're the high priestess' nephew."

"You're new to the coven, so you don't know, but my aunt is a bit of bitch. I got in her way of something she wanted." Lucas shifted to get up. "I gotta go back."

Ari took one arm and Leif took the other. "You can't, not in your condition. Do you have any magic?" She didn't feel any power coming off him. Those magic dampeners were the worst.

"No, but—"

"No buts. We need a plan and you need a bath."

CHAPTER 16

When Ari opened the door to her place, she felt like she'd been transported to another time and place. She stared into the open darkness. No lingering aromas of burned food. The silence nearly toppled her over. Where could Nyah be this time of night?

"Problem?" Leif said with a bit a strain in his voice.

He held Lucas in his arms like a child. By the look on her cousins' face, he was not pleased.

"You can put me down. I can walk," Lucas groused.

"No, there's no problem and no, you can't walk by yourself." Ari waved her hand and the entire room illuminated. "C'mon in."

Leif placed Lucas on the sofa, gently. When Lucas had tried to walk, back at the parking lot, they soon discovered that her cousin's ankles were swollen to the size of grapefruits. It was amazing he'd made it as far as he did to find her.

Ari put the kettle on, then sat back down next to her cousin. Leif sat in the armchair near them.

"When you escaped, did you see where you were? What part of town?" Leif stared at Lucas.

Lucas looked at his hands thoughtfully. "I don't really know. I thought I knew all of the holding facilities." He looked between Ari and Leif. "I have no idea. The blue magic dampeners... had a weird effect on me. They blinded me for hours."

"And your powers?" Ari asked.

"Mine didn't come back, but Luca had just enough to get me out before she passed out."

Ari and Lucas's eyes snapped up at Leif's growl.

"What's wrong?"

"A coven is supposed to be a family. I didn't sign up for this when I joined Black Blood."

Ari couldn't remember the last time he talked so much, if ever. He stood up, and she followed. "Where are you going?"

"Need answers."

Ah, back to the Leif she knew. "And what? You're going to go in freezing everyone? That won't work and you know it."

He stepped closer to her, invading her personal space bubble. "I can be stealthy." He ran a finger from cheek to her bottom lip. "And I can get answers when I need to."

He slid his finger to her chin and lifted it. Suddenly, Ari didn't have control over her body, and she leaned in.

"Hey, you two. Get a room," Lucas said between gags.

Leif lifted one brow as if to say, "It's up to you."

If her place wasn't becoming a Motel 6, then maybe she could've taken him to her bedroom. "Don't look." She waved her hand, and all of the lights went out.

Her hands slid around his neck and she raised up on her tiptoes. This was new for her. She wasn't used to being the shorter person when kissing a guy. His cool hands slid around her waist and pulled her tight to him, before she could think about anything or change her mind, not that she wanted to. His lips touched hers tentatively for one peck, then two more.

Ari moved her hands over both of Leif's cheeks and pulled him in. His lips covered hers and Ari moved to deepen their kiss. A moan filled the room, and she didn't know if it came from him or her. She couldn't really decipher much past the tingling this man caused throughout her body.

"Hey! I'm still here." Lucas called out in the darkness.

Her cousin's voice pulled them out of their own world. They broke the kiss, but not their hold on each other.

"Be careful," Ari whispered.

Leif grunted his assent, then kissed along her neck.

Ari closed her eyes at the tingling sensations vibrating up and down her spine from his touch. It took a lot to keep her train of thought.

"Leif," Ari said, but he continued to kiss her. "Leif, listen to me."

With a huff of annoyance, he pulled away. "I am."

"You know what the coven is like. They will kill you if they think you are betraying them."

"I know. I'll be careful and I'll contact you when I find your cousin." He gave her one last, but long, deep kiss before leaving.

Ari waved her hand as she walked back to her armchair and all the lights came back on.

"So." Lucas grinned. "You and the Prince of Cold?"

Is that what they call him? "That's none of your business," Ari blurted, but warmth slid up her neck.

Lucas threw his hands up. "Hey, hey. I'm happy for you. Especially after the last guy."

A small pillow flew across the room and hit her cousin. "Shut up. You don't need to bring him up."

How could she forget Heath or rather Haviland? He used a glamour to look younger and seduce her to get what he wanted. And then turned out to be the witch running around stealing and murdering witches for their magic. Leif may be cold, but she didn't get the evil vibe from him.

You didn't get it from Heath either. She couldn't stand the little voice in her head. Particularly when it was right.

"Tell me Cuz, how long have you known the magic leech?"

"The what?"

"What were you doing in magic training classes? The guy who nearly killed me? Well, it might have worked if I'd had any magic for him to steal."

Is that what was happening? "But I never sensed magic from him in all the months we've worked together."

"Months?!" Lucas squawked. "Woman, where do you meet these men? You can't see him again!"

"What? Why?"

"First off, you didn't feel magic, because he doesn't have any. He's like a black hole for power. Not to mention, he can also kill you."

Ari found that hard to believe. Jacque was such a gentle person. Well, unless she was in danger, apparently. Granted, she could never see his aura, but she chalked that up to being in the bar. And the funky havoc the lay lines did with magic. And plus, they didn't really hang out, outside of work.

"Lucas, Jacque is one of the nicest people I know. And I get the feeling he doesn't have many friends."

"Shit, no wonder. When he can literally suck the life out of them."

Ari shook her head. No matter what her cousin said, Jacque was her friend. She knew what it was like to be alone with powers that could be destructive. "It doesn't matter, he's my friend. I won't abandon him when he's done nothing wrong to me."

"What about me?"

"Well, truthfully, you did lunge at me." She held up a finger when Lucas opened his mouth to interrupt. "And, you're in this shape because of family, not because of him."

Lucas rolled his eyes, which was a clear sign he was feeling much better. Ari stared at the door and frowned.

"What? He's not coming back tonight. At least, I hope not. I could just imagine the noise…"

"Shut it, boy." Ari laughed as she looked away from the door. "That's not what I was thinking about. I have a friend staying with me and she's usually here. Just kind of worried, that's all."

"Is she hot? Irresistible? You know my type." Lucas flexed his eyebrows up and down in a very Groucho Marx fashion.

"One, ew. And two, no I don't know your type. Thank goddess. She's new to town, but maybe she's finding her way around."

Ari would call Buster, maybe he snatched her away to hang out. But he would have called if he had, right? She walked to the hall closet and pulled out a pillow, sheets, and a comforter. She placed another bottle of water on the side table.

"I'm going to bed, you need anything else?" Ari asked, after fixing the sofa up as a bed.

Lucas pulled the covers up to his neck and shook his head like a little kid. "No, Mommie. All good."

He was a hot mess most of the time, but she loved him. "My friend, she knows about me, but not you guys. So…" Her hand motioned on the side of her mouth as if locking it up.

"Got it. No witchy talk."

Something in Ari made her apprehensive about Nyah knowing more witches just yet. She turned to leave, then came back and kissed him on the forehead. "We'll get Rum back. No matter what."

"I know," Lucas said, then his lips tightened. He turned over before the tears welling up in his eyes could fall. "Wuv ya, Cuz."

The words came out muffled and Lucas would never say 'love' anyway, but she heard him. She felt the same way about him.

CHAPTER 17

An ear-piercing scream woke Ari. Couldn't she just have one morning where she woke up like a normal person? Maybe roused by the smell of bacon and coffee? Even morning sex? Well, she'd have to start with getting any sex.

Sunlight beamed through the window blinds, and Ari walked into a standoff. Nyah held a knife on the half-naked Lucas on the couch. When did he strip down?

"Ari, we have an intruder." Nyah poked the kitchen blade at her cousin's chest.

"I see." Ari stood with her arms crossed.

"Cuz, tell her to stop pointing that thing at me."

When Ari didn't say anything, Nyah took that as 'take out' the stranger and lunged. Lucas climbed over the back of the sofa, leaving the sheets and comforter. As naked as the day he was born, Lucas, flicked his hand out and his would-be attacker flew through the air and hit the wall.

"Lucas!" Ari ran to the downed Nyah.

"She was going to kill me." Lucas huffed from behind her.

"You okay?" Ari helped Nyah stand up. "She wasn't going to kill you," she said to Lucas.

"I was," Nyah whispered.

Ari was shocked to hear that, as she looked around, there wasn't a crack in the wall, so maybe no body parts were broken. The only casualty was a broken herb pot. Nyah knocked the dirt off of her legs and arms.

"I'm okay, but he—" Nyah pointed then her eyes went as big as baseballs before she whipped around. "He shouldn't be here."

Ari turned to see Lucas, near the sofa, without a stitch of clothing on. She turned her head slightly to avoid Lucas' full monty, then spoke, "My dearest cousin, could you please put something on, and I will introduce you to my roommate."

"Um, yeah, I need to borrow something."

"Good goddess," Ari mumbled. "Nyah, could you please sit at the table and don't attack him again? Annoying as he is, he's still family."

Nyah walked sideways to the long wooden table, keeping her back to Lucas.

"Come on." Ari walked to her bedroom and Lucas followed.

A few minutes later, the shower started, and Ari walked straight to the kitchen and put the kettle on.

A grueling thirty minutes later, Lucas emerged smelling like her peony and rose petal soap. He was shirtless, even though Ari gave him one. The towel moved vigorously over his head.

"Goddess above and demon below, I feel like a new man." Lucas lowered the towel.

Ari spit out her tea. "What did you do?"

"What?" He ran his hand over his head. "I think it looks nice."

Ari circled around him. The once chestnut, long wavy locks were a memory. She ran her fingers front to back over his scalp. The soft bristles reminded her of peach fuzz.

"Ari, it's just hair. It'll grow back."

"I know, but…" The chestnut locks were midway his back. The longest he ever let it grow.

"No buts." He cut her off. "I couldn't get it untangled. This was simpler. Now introduce me to your knife-wielding roomie."

Nyah stood as they approached, but still averted her eyes.

"Nyah, I'd like to introduce you to my cousin, Lucas," Ari said with a hand wave towards him. "Lucas, Nyah."

Nyah held her hand out to him.

Lucas cleared his throat. "You said her name is, Nyah?" When Ari nodded, he pulled her across the room, out of earshot. "Is that *his Nyah?*"

Ari looked at Nyah with an innocent, it's okay smile, then nodded.

Lucas opened his mouth like he was going to speak, then snapped it shut and walked away with his fist in his mouth. He made the trip to her twice before he spoke.

"Are you crazy?" he said in an angry whisper. "And why does she look like Royal O'Malley?"

"You know who Royal is?" She shook her head. "Never mind, that part was an accident. But she looks totally different now."

He lifted a brow with a smirk on his lip. She clearly read it to mean, "Really?"

"Ari?" Nyah called from other side of the room.

"Sorry. We're being rude." Ari called back, then turned to Lucas and whispered, "Look, just be nice. She's nothing like Haviland."

Lucas held his hands up in surrender. "Fine, fine."

Ari lead the way back with a smile. "My cousin has a condition."

Lucas stood behind her with his arms crossed over his chest.

Nyah extended her hand, then snatched it back. "He is unwell?"

"Very much so. He has Foot-in-mouth disease. It's not fatal, but it's bad when meeting people."

Lucas squawked behind her. "Oh, I see how it is."

"Will I get this 'foot-in-mouth' sickness?" Nyah began to absent-mindedly rub her arm.

"No. I'm sure you'll be okay," Ari said grinning, then turned to speak to them both. "I have to leave for a little bit."

They both whined their disapproval. Ari covered her ears until they stopped.

"I won't be gone long. You guys can survive without me for a little while."

Nyah yawned. Lucas frowned.

"Go to bed. I'll be back before you know it."

Nyah shook her head to protest. "I can go…" Then her mouth opened wide when another more powerful yawn took over.

"You can go to bed. See ya later."

Nyah walked towards the bedrooms. Ari grabbed her leather messenger bag. Lucas blocked the door just as she reached for it.

"What is it now?"

"Where are you going?" Lucas eyed her friend suspiciously.

"None of your business, *Dad.* Why you wanna know?"

"What are we going to do about my sister?" Lucas leaned back on the door.

He really wasn't going to let her leave. Her bag slid down her arm. "We can't do anything till we know where they're holding her. Once Leif gets that info, we can go in."

"Can't we send Remy in or something?"

The desperation in his voice broke her heart. "Remy hasn't been around much. As a matter of fact, he's been out of pocket for a week or so. I don't know what's going on with him."

"He might have a girl?" Lucas winked.

"Ew. That's just wrong on so many levels. I'll be back."

Lucas eased off the door. "What about her?"

"What about her?"

He had the nerve to look sheepish.

"If you don't trust her that much, lock yourself in my room. I'm sure she won't possess you and make you do unspeakable things to her."

Ari heard him say, "She wish," as she walked out the door.

CHAPTER 18

The Hot Toddy was a fusion tea/coffee/speakeasy with karaoke kind of bar and Ari's favorite place to get a drink. Even though she was an unofficial tea aficionado, this place made the best Irish coffee. It wasn't very busy that morning. A few people along the bar and two girlfriends giggling in the bay window seats. They were in her and Leise's favorite spot. Being here just made her miss her friend that much more.

In the back corner, near the restroom, someone sat with their hoodie pulled over their head and fingerless gloves wrapped around a king-kong sized mug of something. She would have picked a place with more sun, and maybe a view, but she got there late. *Damn family.*

"Jacque?" Ari stood at the edge of a small round bistro-style table.

He lifted his head and pulled the hood back. A mess of wavy, jet black hair flopped out. "Hey."

Red-rimmed sapphire blue eyes with a nice set of black luggage underneath looked up at her. Ari pulled out the chair across from his to sit and he jumped up and ran around behind her.

"I'm sor… sorry. Forgot my… my manners." As he pushed her

chair in, it scraped along the hardwood floor, causing a few people to look in their direction. He lumbered back to his seat.

"You okay?"

He shook his head. "Is your friend okay?"

"He's actually my cousin and yeah, he's much better."

"Can I get you something?" A female voice said from next to the table.

"Um, yeah. An extra special Irish coffee." Ari knew she would need something stronger than English Breakfast this morning.

The waitress held a metal camp-style coffee pot. "You want me to top that off?" The pot moved toward Jacque's mug. He leaned back and the young woman filled up his cup. A steady stream of steam rose and Jacque inhaled.

"I'll get that order right out."

Jacque didn't add anything to his coffee, he blew on it then sipped it. He didn't say anything and neither did Ari. This was something he needed to say in his own time, she wasn't going to rush him.

"What makes it ex… extra?" He glanced up.

Ari smiled. "Two shots of Jameson."

His shoulders moved. She was pretty sure he laughed.

"Anything else?" The waitress placed a tall, clear glass mug with a frothy, light brown coffee in front of Ari.

The rich, coffee aroma assailed her senses. "No, this is great." She reached for the sugar dispenser and stirred a teaspoon in.

Ari lifted her mug and waited. Jacque's eyes widened just before he scrambled to lift his glass.

"Here's to friends and friendship." She lightly clinked her mug into his, then took one sip and smiled. "That's some good stuff right there."

He sipped and for the first time this morning, his two dimples emerged.

"You really want to be my friend?"

Ari reached out and touched him. "I am your friend. Now, tell me."

A tear splashed on their intertwined hands. Jacque quickly wiped any other liquid betrayers away.

"I was… was born without any magic of my own. What you saw me do." He cleared his throat. "Wow, this is really hard. I've never told anyone outside the coven. I'm what our witch mythology calls, a psyphon."

CHAPTER 19

The skeleton key jingled as Ari knocked on the White Cauldron's front door. Elizabeth gave it to her when she signed on to help train the young witches.

"Hello." Ari walked in slowly. "Anyone home?"

"Why do you ask that every time you drop by?" Elizabeth appeared in the library area of the shop. "I'm always here."

Ari walked towards her. "Well, I don't know. You could be doing something personal."

"Like what, pray tell?"

"I don't know. Maybe walking around naked or…" Ari looked out the window. "Outside."

Elizabeth nodded, then strolled towards a wingback chair in the library section of the store. "If that's your subtle way of asking if I took the potion, that would be a no."

"Why not? I'm sure it'll work."

"The city has changed a lot in the last 131 years." Elizabeth kept her eyes averted as she tapped her fingers on her skirt.

Ari nodded. "Okay." It was clear the house entity was scared and would have to leave the building in her own time. "Have you heard about the strange illness going around?"

Elizabeth nodded. "The reports are distressing. Why do you ask?"

"I don't know. It seems unnatural."

"I have no idea what it could be. Just be careful out there. You don't want to fall victim to it."

"I will." Ari nodded. "In other news, the coven kidnapped my cousins."

"It's actually an abduction when adults are taken."

"Fine. Whatever. My cousins were abducted and beaten."

"Goodness. This story sounds like we might need a drink."

Elizabeth walked to the bookcase shelf filled with color-filled potion bottles. She moved them to the side and pulled out a diamond etched bottle filled with a caramel-colored liquid and two small glasses. She poured two fingers worth in each glass and handed one to Ari.

Elizabeth held the glass out and Ari clinked hers.

"Cheers," they both said at the same time.

"Now, tell me what happened," Elizabeth said after she took a sip.

Ari sipped the liquid courage and made a face. "Whew, that some strong stuff." She sat the glass down on the side table. "Lucas and Rum were taken because they helped us."

"With the twitch training?"

Ari shook her head. "No, the battle with Haviland. My mother found out about Haviland's ability and that they were there."

"And she wants him." Elizabeth put her whiskey on the side table.

"She wants it all. Him, his spell book. Probably, his blood too knowing her." She took a long draw from her whiskey. Made another face. She was not a straight whiskey drinker.

"Power," Elizabeth added.

"And that's not the best part, she also wants me to marry some guy from a New Orleans coven."

"Come again? Do you mean an arranged marriage?" Elizabeth leaned forward.

Ari always found that phrase to be funny, but she couldn't even muster up any laughter today.

"No one does that anymore. It's barbaric!" Elizabeth's fists clinched when she stood to pace.

Ari looked at the woman with renewed interest. She wasn't sure if she'd ever really seen her upset about anything. "I told you my cousins were abducted and tortured, but it's the marriage thing that's got you worked up?"

Elizabeth didn't speak for a long moment. "You know I was married."

Ari nodded.

"It was arranged by my father to his best friend's son."

It all became clear to Ari why this touched a nerve. "You didn't know him at all before the marriage?"

"I saw him in social settings. Dinner parties, dances. We even had conversations about his scientific pursuits." Elizabeth finished her whiskey and poured another.

"And you couldn't say no." Ari made it a statement, not a question.

"Not back then. I was not quite ready to be a spinster or worse, disowned."

Ari couldn't even imagine not having any choice in decisions about her own life. "I'm sorry."

Elizabeth wiped the lone tear. "Pish-posh." She cleared her throat. "That was a long time ago. Now, if you don't want to marry the guy. Don't."

"I have no intention of it. Hell, I haven't even seen him."

"We can't worry about a guy you haven't met yet. Your cousins, that's the real concern right now. You have a plan to get them back?" She sat back down and sipped her whiskey.

"Lucas busted out. They still have Rum. We're waiting on info before we go in," Ari said.

"Who from? Is it a reliable source? Please say you didn't send in Remy?"

"No. He's MIA right now. I'm starting to get a little worried."

"He's a ghost. What's the worst that could happen?" Elizabeth smiled.

"I guess you're right."

Elizabeth patted her knee. "You were about to tell me your source?"

Ari could feel her face heat up. Not sure whether she blushed or not, that remained to be seen. She lifted her hand to cover her smile. "Yeah, I trust him."

"What's that look?" Elizabeth leaned in. "What's his name? Out with it." She leaned back and crossed her hands over her lap.

"This guy. He abducted me a couple of weeks ago."

"What? Where do you find these men?"

Everybody was a comedian. "No, no. He's not a bad guy." Ari waved it off.

"Clearly," Elizabeth mumbled under her breath.

"Really," Ari gushed. "That whole kidnapping thing was under orders of the coven. Before I got to know him. Leif is actually a really nice guy. Considerate. A little broody, but what guy isn't."

"You say, the coven told him to abduct you," Elizabeth said meaningfully. When Ari nodded, she continued. "Who's to say he's not… what do the kids say? Ah, yes, hooking up with you by order of the coven?"

"He's not." Ari shook her head emphatically.

"How do you know?"

Ari jumped up. "I just do, okay." Her voice reached a new octave.

She didn't yell, and they weren't fighting. She didn't think Leif was acting, but what did she really know. He could cook, a great kisser, but doesn't like to talk. He's searching for something.

"I'm sorry," Elizabeth touched Ari's hand.

Ari blinked out of her deep thoughts of Leif. "No, I understand."

If Leise or anyone else would have told her this story, she would have reacted the same way as Elizabeth.

"I just don't want you to get hurt. Bring him around. I'd like to meet him. Does he like tea?" Elizabeth said with a smile.

Ari grinned. Her first cup of tea with the shop owner contained a truth spell. "I'm sure he does, but…" It seemed wrong to subject him to a lie detector test without him knowing.

"I won't hurt him." Elizabeth held out her pinky. "Pinky swear."

The pinky swear is a light binding spell and a serious thing. It's mostly used by young witches and parents with small kids because they do no real damage if someone doesn't keep their word. You might only lose your favorite pen or waste red punch on a white dress. Magic always has a price, even small ones.

Ari's pinky hooked through Elizabeth's. "Fine."

"I hope to see you both soon," Elizabeth said with a smile.

"Yes." Ari grabbed her stuff.

"How's your houseguest?" Elizabeth asked from behind her.

Ari turned around with a frown. "Girl!" She took a deep breath. "I understand she comes from a time that didn't have indoor plumbing, but she lives in that bathroom. I don't know what she does in there all day. I like her, I really do, but momma needs her space back."

"What are you going to do?" Elizabeth held the door.

"I don't know but it's not like I can let her out to work at the local Dairy Queen."

"She doesn't want to spend eternity with him?"

Ari knew Elizabeth didn't even like saying his name. She felt it gave him too much power. "Haviland? Nope, seems like the ship has sailed on that love. She said she couldn't possibly be with a monster like that."

Elizabeth cringed. "How did he take it?"

"I haven't seen him. Thought he might need a little time." Ari didn't want to see Haviland after he got dumped. Let alone reveal his lady love has been living it up without him.

"In other words, you're scared to see your ex?"

"No," Ari said. "That's not it." It's not like she could ever forget him.

"Let me know how that goes. And once you find out about Rum, let me know how we can help. We will help you get her back.

The girls love her and a few of the guys have taken to her." She opened her arms and gave Ari a hug. "Merry meet and safe travels."

Ari walked out, but she didn't head home. Her ghost radar was usually off the charts this time of year. It had been quiet. Too quiet. And now Remy had gone missing. None of this was normal. She needed answers and knew of only one place to get them.

She needed to have a conversation with the dead.

CHAPTER 20

The swing on the huge oak tree in the middle of the Woodland Glen cemetery stopped moving, but the swing seat hovered in the air.

Ari stood motionless. "Krista? You here?"

The young ghost had not made herself visible yet. The wind whistled and time seemed to falter. Then gravity took the swing, and the dead leaves rustled with the rhythm of someone walking.

Arms folded over her dark dress. The young ghost stamped her foot. "Where have you been? Didn't you get my message?"

"No. What're you talking about?"

"I told Remy to tell you," Krista said.

Ari shook her head. "I haven't seen him for a few days."

"No, no, no," Krista said through her hands as she paced away. "She must have him too."

"Who must have him? Krista talk to me." Ari followed behind the girl.

"There have been some strange things going on out here."

"Okay, I'm here now. You know you can tell me."

"That's just it. I can't." Krista walked away kicking at a rock. Her Mary Janes ghosted right through it.

The young ghost moved around angrily. Ari could tell she wanted to say something, but couldn't. "Is it a secret?" Ari clasped her hands together. "I can keep a secret."

"Kinda. Oh—" Krista jumped around. "This part's no secret. Your friend has been hanging out with a bad witch."

"Who? Remy? What witch?"

Krista opened her mouth, but then it snapped shut.

Was her mother up to something? Maybe that's why she wants to merge with the New Orleans clan. She'd heard stories about some of their witches' magic. Darker than anything she could dream of. Right up Erissa's alley.

"You want to tell me but can't. Am I close?"

Krista tapped her nose.

A spell, then. Not many witches could control ghosts. A necromancer could, but she didn't know any of those. "Did the bad witch do this to all the ghosts?"

Krista nodded. "But we can talk about anything else. The weather, how busy Halloween's going to be around here."

Ari nodded in agreement, cemeteries were always—. She gasped when she got what the girl was really saying.

Krista threw her hands up. "And you're supposed to be the adult. I wished you would have visited sooner." Krista waved at her sealed lips.

"I'm sorry, it won't happen again. Maybe I should visit you every night."

Krista shook her head. "Not safe for anyone around here. Especially if ghosts are going to—" Her mouth sealed up. She stomped around, no doubt cursing up a storm, slapping her sealed lips.

The entire scene about broke Ari's heart. "Calm down."

She got in the path of the angry ghost and braced herself. Ghosts couldn't possess her. Instead of passing through her, Ari's body responded like a brick wall. Krista bumped into her chest and they both fell on their butts.

"What the hay, Ari?"

If the little girl could breathe, she might have passed out she was so worked up. "I don't like seeing you like that. We won't talk about stuff you can't talk about."

Krista stood up, straightened her dress with a firm shake, then went back to her swing. "I know more you don't."

"Don't say it. Let me guess. The bad witches promised to make you alive again." Krista nodded. "You know it's dark magic, and nothing good can come from that."

Krista's head lifted like a hound scenting the air. "You need to go."

"What's happening, Krista?" Ari looked around frantically but saw nothing. Then the hairs on her arm stood at attention. She knew that feeling all too well.

Black magic.

Krista's hands covered her ears and squinted her eyes in horror. It looked more like pain. "They're calling us." She fell forward, and on instinct, Ari tried to catch her. The swing kept moving, but Ari's hands were empty. Krista had disappeared.

CHAPTER 21

The streets of Houston went by in a blur on Ari's way home. But when the car stopped, she wasn't at her place. She found herself looking at an old two level, French Quarter style apartment complex on the westside.

Her fingers meandered over the wrought iron fleur-de-lis gate as she walked. Leif's door opened before she even knocked.

She put her hands in her pockets and rocked back on her feet. "Hey."

"Hey," Leif replied in the same casual tone, then ran his fingers through his hair.

They stood in an uncomfortable silence for longer than she'd liked. At this point, she feared she'd made a mistake. When she opened her mouth to say she was sorry for waking him, he stepped back opening the door wider. She crossed the threshold.

Ari looked around the small, but immaculate apartment. It seemed larger the last time she was there. A pair of slippers were at the entrance, she slid off her flats and put them on. She would never hear the end of it if she tracked dirt in on his arctic white shag rug or scratched his black hardwood floors. It almost scared her to sit on the white leather sectional.

"Coffee?" Leif asked, as he rummaged around in the open kitchen.

She had only ever seen this man in a suit, but the midnight blue silk pajama bottoms hung nicely on his hips. They were crumpled like he'd been laying down, but the pristine white t-shirt clued her in that he'd just put it on. She was pretty sure he slept half naked.

"No, thank you," Ari said, as she sat. "Sorry, if I woke you."

"No worries." He looked at her from over the counter. "You know, I feel like some tea."

"You didn't strike me as a tea guy." Ari admired the coffee table. Ran her fingers over the iron scroll pattern.

"I'm part Asian, you know."

She looked up and tsked. "You know that means nothing. Stereotypes are the devil's pride and joy."

"Fine. My mom always made tea when I lived with her. I hated it at first, but as I got older. I don't know… maybe I do it to remember her."

Did he just string along two sentences? Ari wanted to know more about this enigmatic man but erred on the side of caution when asking questions. She didn't want him to clam up.

"Oh, I'm sorry. I didn't mean to—"

He shook his head. "She's not dead. She's just… my eomeoni is complicated." The kettle whistled.

"Oh-ma-nee? Is that your mother's name?"

Leif didn't answer. She thought maybe she'd asked one question too many. He came in carrying a tray with a white porcelain tea pot and small handleless cups. He placed it on the glass and iron coffee table in front of the long section of the seating area. This reminded her of the first time she had tea with Elizabeth. Her friend would like him.

"We need to let it steep." He turned to her. "Eomeoni means mother, and she had to give me up when my hair did this." He touched the ends of it.

Ari loved his hair. She thought he'd dyed it when she first met him. "I think it's beautiful."

"Yeah, beautiful," Leif grumbled.

Ari thought he was about to spit after saying the word. Note to self, no comments about his hair.

"Where I come from it's a sign of misfortune." He poured two cups of the light green liquid. "I'm a bastard, and for my mother's sake, they accepted me, but just barely. Then this happened. My mother sent me to my father in upstate New York. Now, drink your tea." He blew on his before taking a sip.

As he told the story, she didn't realize the cup had been poised at her lips the entire time. She followed his lead and took a sip. The pale green tea had bits of plant floating in it. The flavor seemed familiar.

"What kind of tea is this?"

"It's called ssukcha." He took another sip. "Or mugwort tea."

"I can taste it now. It's kind of like the mugwort I use, but a little more bitter. I like it." She took another sip and held out her cup.

"So, what's up with Ella Grace?"

The pot faltered, and he wasted tea on the rug and table. "Sorry." He jumped up and rushed to the kitchen. He came back with a towel and cleaned up the mess.

"I didn't mean to pry. It's just, she has that special name for you. I don't know, you guys seem close, that's all. You don't have to tell me." She felt like such a girl in that moment. Sure, she wanted to know him, but was she truly jealous?

Leif shook his head. "It's nothing like that. I've known her for a few years. I used to work security at her father's medical facility. Some guys broke in one day and started shooting up the place. I got her out of the way. Took a bullet."

"What?! Oh, my. You saved her. That explains it." Well, no wonder the girl is in love with him, she thought.

"Not a big deal."

"Did you not use your powers because you worked for dismages?"

He nodded, then motioned toward her tea. "You done?"

She nodded, then turned the cup up, finishing the last of her tea. "Yes." He collected the cups and tray and carried it to the kitchen.

When he came back into the room, he asked. "What brought you over here tonight?" He looked at his watch, then said, "This morning?"

Honestly, talking to him made her forget whatever was on her mind. But it all came back with a vengeance. But she didn't want to get into it. "Anything on Rum?"

He stared at her, almost as if he was looking through her, before he shook his head. "Nothing concrete, but something's going on. I can feel it."

"Your witchy intuition?"

He smiled. "Something like that."

She looked at her watch. "I should go."

"No," Leif said with a smirk. "You woke me up, the least you can do is stay till I fall back asleep."

She eyed him dubiously. "And how can I do that?"

He scooted to the far end of the couch, stretched out and held his arms wide.

"If I must," she said, as she crawled along the couch. Her inner cat woman was alive and well.

"You must, you must," he said the next line with a big smile.

She settled between his legs and in his arms. "You know that movie?"

"Who doesn't know that movie?" He kissed her temple, then pulled her tighter.

She shivered. "You run a little cooler than most guys."

An arctic blast whooshed through the room. "No talking about other men in my presence."

She laughed at his show of jealousy and snuggled closer to him. "Got it. No other men."

Leif leaned to the side and lifted her face to his. He didn't say anything. He didn't have to. Soft lips ravished her in a blitz of tongue and teeth. It was all she could do to just hang on. Leif kissed her like a man possessed and she liked it.

Bliss. That was a word Ari had rarely used. But Leif had a way of making her forget everything. And could the guy kiss. She smiled just thinking about it. She hadn't made out with a guy on the couch since high school. They'd watched the sunrise, then she came home. He offered to cook, but she wanted to make sure Lucas and Nyah hadn't destroyed her place.

What was going on in her city? The mug in her hand had gone stone cold and she hadn't taken one sip. The glass door slid open behind her.

"Morning," Lucas said after a long yarn. "How long you been up?"

"I never went to sleep." She placed the mug of cold tea on the small mosaic table next to a potted chamomile plant.

He took a seat. "The Houston skyline is beautiful. I never paid much attention before."

"It's ok." After the strange conversation with Krista she felt this was the quiet before the storm. She wanted to talk to someone about it, but she didn't have any real information.

"Hey."

His words snapped her back to the here and now. "Yeah."

"What got you with that scowl on your face?"

Her cheeks hurt from faking the smile and she wasn't pulling it off. "There's so much going on in this city that I don't know about. Do you know if Erissa has added a necromancer to the coven?"

"There have been a lot of new people and changes at the coven, but I can't say that I've met one."

"And the new coven?"

"What are you getting at?" Lucas turned towards her. "You know something?"

"No, not really."

He looked at her for a long minute. "When you *really* have something, you'll tell me, right?"

"Of course."

"So, um, Cuz. You gone drink that?" He pointed at the tea.

"No. It's cold."

"Seriously, Ari?" He rolled his eyes. "Just warm it up, please."

She hardly used her firepower for mundane things like this anymore. She put her finger into the cold liquid and swirled it around. Within a minute steam rose and the light orange citrusy aroma with hints of bergamot filled the air.

Ari shook her finger of excess tea, then tasted it. "That extra sugar I added was free."

"I'm just going to pretend I didn't see that and ignore the fact that this tasty tea had anything to do with your finger." He sipped it, then inhaled the next two gulps.

She pulled one foot onto the edge of her chair and laid her head on her knees. With her eyes closed, she let the morning sun warm her.

"Have you heard from him?"

Ari nodded her head.

"And..."

"He's okay, but doesn't know anything yet."

He nodded. "I hope it's soon."

"I know. I want to get Rum back as much as you do. I've wanted to storm in and demand they hand her over since you told me. But when we do get her back, have you thought about what you guys are going to do? You can't go back. At least I wouldn't think you would want to."

"I know I can't and pretty sure Luca Bea won't either. I don't know where we can go." He turned up the mug and finished the tea.

"We'll figure it out. You're my family and the only ones who care about me besides Leise." She reached out and grabbed his hand.

"Speaking of which, how's she doing with Brandon?"

"It's Brennan. And they are doing great. On Leise's last postcard, she said they were going to check out some small islands near Ireland."

"When are they coming back?"

"I don't know, they're still searching for his homeland. I miss her so much, but hopefully not too much longer."

"What are your plans today?"

"I was thinking about heading over to Tea & Tarot. I have a few people I need to see."

"Can I come? I love your place, but I'm getting kinda claustrophobic."

"So, this sudden need to commune with nature has nothing to do with Topaz."

"None what-so-ever." He held up his fingers like a scout. "Scout's honor."

"You weren't a scout."

"And this is not about her." Hand over his heart. "Swear to the goddess above. It's all about those pretty little thong panties she wears."

CHAPTER 22

After a hot shower and Nyah's partially burned toast and scorched eggs, Ari and Lucas headed out to her Tea and Tarot booth in downtown Houston. Nyah declined to join them, from fear of contracting Lucas's Foot-in-mouth disease.

She'd texted a few of her clients before heading out just in case they were in the area and could pick up their orders. If not, Ari would deliver them.

A warm breeze whistled by Ari. By the time she looked up, a young woman with long legs was holding down her skirt. Lucas' finger whirled around in a small circle, moving air around his intended target.

"Lucas," Ari angry whispered, as she covered his finger. "Stop that."

The gust stopped abruptly, lowering Topaz's skirt, but she held it in a firm grip as she walked along the green.

"You're no fun, Cuz," Lucas whined.

Topaz shook out her flowy skirt once she made it to her booth.

"The winds down here are insane. Just never know what they are going to do," Topaz said in her rich as caramel Texas drawl.

"You are so right. The wind is crazy," Ari said.

"Ari is that you?" Topaz leaned to see around the black and green can art mobiles. "Good to see you, Stranger. Goodness, it's been forever since I saw you last," Topaz said, after giving Ari a hug.

"You remember my cousin, Lucas." Ari waved towards him.

"How could I forget such a handsome face." Instead of a wave or handshake, she pulled him in for a hug.

The smile on his face was pure bliss. Air began to billow under her skirt. Ari made a strangling motion behind Topaz. Then the wind suddenly stopped.

Topaz pulled away, checking her skirt. "See what I'm saying? This wind. Madness, right?"

"Absolutely." Ari nodded.

After getting set-up, Lucas went to walk around, and about fifteen minutes later her first client showed up. The woman could have been mistaken for Death herself. With black jeans, black sweater and a long black coat. The deep burgundy eye shadow and lipstick were in deep contrast to her pale skin. With all of that, the woman's aura seemed very familiar. The bright yellow of positive energy, sprinkled with pink highlights of joy seemed to be in a battle with the storm gray ring of dread that seemed to be trying to take her over.

"Ari, where have you been?"

Ari knew that high pitched, valley-girl voice, knew those eyes, and knew that dark cloud of despair that followed this woman around. "Brittania?"

"I go by Britt, now. Have I really changed that much?" Brittania looked down at herself. "I know the clothes are a little dark. I was going for something different."

Mission accomplished. "Why?" Ari began to shuffle her tarot cards.

The woman looked extremely young all of the sudden as she fidgeted with the buttons on her coat. "When you weren't here. I sorta went to a new person."

Ari nodded. "Okay, and what did this person tell you?" She already had a feeling where this was going. "Let me guess you needed a change. There was a new you waiting to get out."

"Well, yeah, but he used words like evolve and transformation." She used her hands to illustrate each word.

"And do you like the transformation of Britt?" Ari spread the cards out in an arc.

"Yeah, sure," Brittania said, with a little too much glee.

Ari didn't believe it for a minute. "Pull a card." The cards wouldn't lie.

Instead of drawing a card from the middle, like most people tended to do. She picked a card that was sticking out a bit to her far right.

"You said a guy read your cards. Where was this?" Ari flipped over the chosen card.

"Down on the other end." Brittania pointed towards the long path of tables and pop-up tents.

Ari tapped the card in front of her. "Britt, this card says something else."

Brittania stared at the card. Running her finger over the card, touching the face of the girl crying into a blanket on her bed, the nine daggers above the window, and the trapped bat. "That's me, every night."

The words were so soft that Ari almost didn't hear them. "Let me help you. This is no way to live: fear, stress, the needless anxiety."

Tears began to stream down Brittania's face as she nodded.

"You don't have to tell me. Just know I'm here." Ari reached her hand out, palm up.

The young woman looked up with red-rimmed eyes, then finally took Ari's hand. "Help me. I don't want to be this anymore. I'm hearing voices. I feel like I'm losing—" She exhaled. "You understand."

Ari squeezed her hand, then pulled back. "Pick another card."

"This is not like our normal readings." Brittania pulled a card from the middle.

Ari flipped the card over and smiled.

"Is that a witch? I'm not a witch, am I?" Brittania leaned in, then sat ram rod up straight.

"No," Ari tapped the card just above the young woman in the witch's hat sitting near the boiling cauldron on the card. "You are moving past bad things. It means, you have a new future ahead. But you have to see your way through one more test. Now, pick one more." She did and Ari flipped it over.

Brittania smiled. "That looks like a good card."

Ari returned her smile. "You'll meet a soft-spoken man who loves nature and animals."

"What?!" Brittania yelped, then lowered her voice. "Is this my love card? Where is he?"

"Goddess, no. This talks about who you might meet in the future."

"But you're sure, it specifically shows me meeting a man?" Brittania began to touch her neck, then face.

"Britt, calm down. You're not likely to meet him in the next two-seconds."

"Brittania."

"What?" Ari wasn't sure what had just happened.

"You just said that I was moving forward." She nodded like a decision had been made. "I am Brittania Thomasina Fitzmorgan. And there's a man in my future." She jumped up.

"Wait." Ari reached into the plastic bin under the table. She rummaged until she found the right bag. "Here. It should help you sleep."

Brittania opened the brown paper bag and inhaled. "This smells so good."

"It's agrimony and lavender, with a few other things. Leave it near your bedside."

"Ari, thank you. Don't stay away so long. The others didn't help me, they only told me what I wanted to hear. I know that now."

It felt good to know her work meant something. To know that she was helping people. Her phone buzzed on the bin under the table. She waved bye to one cheerful client before answering.

"Hello. Hello, I can't hear you." The voice spoke quickly in hushed tones. Ari looked at the screen, then listened again. "You're going to have to slow down. Tell me again what happened." The line went dead.

All she could make out was that 'something bad happened' and 'you need to get here now.'

"Who was that?" Lucas sat down across from her.

"I have to go." Ari grabbed her bag. "Something's happened at the senior facility."

CHAPTER 23

Ravenswood Arms had always been a residence for active seniors. Not quite fraternity/sorority living for the older set, but lively enough. Ari and Lucas didn't walk into a lively place at all.

The garden. Empty.

The front desk. Empty.

Lucas looked around quickly. "Cuz, interesting place this is. Is it always this… rousing?"

"Can't you feel it?"

She had to consider that he might not be able to feel the dark magic. It had always been a normal part of his life. Besides he'd only gotten his powers back a few days ago.

Lucas waved his hand slowly through the air. "I don't feel anything."

Ari's skin crawled with the amount of dark magical energies flowing throughout this building. Then one soul appeared.

Nurse Frankie in white scrubs. She pointed up.

"She's up here." They ran past the elevators up the stairs.

"Aracely?!" Ari banged on the door. "Are you in there?"

"Ari? How do I know it's really you?" A dubious, lightly accented voice called through the door. "What do I call you?"

"Aracely, I can't remember. You know I can't speak Spanish worth a damn."

"Then I can't open this door, demonia," Aracely said with a growl.

"Did she just call me a demon?"

Lucas laughed. "See, you do know Spanish."

"Shut up and let me think."

Lucas tapped his chin. "There's señorita, mamacita, margarita, and my personal favorite, tequila." Snaps his fingers. "Ah, puta. I hear that all the time."

"I bet you do. I know enough to know that that one's bad." She laid her palm on the door. "We've talked about many things, the boys, your family. Familia," she smiled. "And you would say, Mija. That's it! Mija."

The door opened as if she'd said the magic word. "Mija, you remind me of mi abuela." Ari finished. She wrapped her arms around the woman. "Are you okay?" She touched the woman's cheek, then arms. When she nodded, Ari moved behind her. "We have to get out of here."

Aracely pushed the red joystick and her new wheels lurched forward. "No time for that, Mija. Vámonos!"

Ari held back her smile. "Aracely, that's not your normal wheelchair." The four-wheeled red rascal scooter even had a basket in the front.

"I needed something with some speed." She stopped abruptly outside the door. She fumbled for her necklace. "Back!"

"No, no." Ari lowered the tiger eye necklace she'd given Aracely for protection. "He's okay. That's my cousin, Lucas."

"Mi Dios. You almost gave me a heart attack."

They hurried downstairs and Nurse Frankie pointed away from the exit.

"Where are you going?" Aracely stopped.

"I think we need to check in here before we go."

Her feet felt as heavy as anvils. No, she didn't want to look. Aracely's new wheelchair whipped past her and she made it to the entertainment room first. Luscious and Michael was all she'd said as she rolled out of sight.

Ari turned the corner to find a full, quiet room. Body after body of healthcare workers, residents, and staff lay on the floor, in chairs, on tables. Luscious and Michael lay sprawled out of their seats, looking anything but alive.

"Luscious?" Ari pressed her fingers to his neck. If he wasn't, she could barely tell.

"Is he?" Aracely asked from the door.

Ari checked Michael, placed her finger under his nose, then looked him over for visible wounds. "I think it's that illness that going around."

"The one I just saw on TV," Lucas chimed in. "Crazy dismage diseases."

"I don't think it is," Ari said as she slowly moved her hand over a nurse in pink scrubs on the floor. "This is magic."

"Man, don't tell me. I don't even want to know. Let's just get out of here." Lucas said backing up.

"Freeze!"

Ari's head snapped up and Lucas lifted his hands up.

"Ma'am, are you okay?" The police officer said to Aracely but kept the gun pointed towards the others.

"Put that gun away," Aracely admonished. "They came here to rescue me."

More armed police officers walked in with guns drawn. Lucas lifted a brow and wiggled his fingers. Ari slowly motioned her head left to right.

"Officer, please. Let me explain," Ari began.

"Why am I not surprised?" A familiar voice sounded through the crowd of blue.

Ari wished she could become invisible and walk out. Instead of a bad penny, she was starting to think of him as a bad case of foot fungus. You forget you have it until it shows up. "Detective Westin."

"Ms. Mason, why is it," he spoke low enough that only she could hear, "when weird shit happens in this town you are right in the middle of it?"

That was really the pot calling the kettle. He crowded her personal space but she wasn't backing up. "I came because a friend called me."

He grunted. "What do you know about this?" He pointed around towards the lifeless bodies.

"We just got here. I found her upstairs in her room. We walked in to see this and I checked to see if they were alive." Because he would surely believe a ghost led her to Aracely and the bodies.

"Did it occur to you to call the police?"

"Well, obviously someone did. I just wanted to get out. This is all too creepy." Ari rubbed her arms like she had a chill. She didn't have one, but pretending to be helpless seemed to be his trigger. Helpless women. And the only way to get him to back up most times, but not for very long.

"I find it hard to believe this is the creepiest thing you've ever seen," Detective Westin mumbled.

"If that's all, we'd like to get out of here," Ari said, ignoring his words.

"I need to ask them some questions." He pointed towards Aracely and Lucas.

"Fine. Can you do that somewhere else? This has to be torture for Ms. Aracely."

He frowned, like he was ready to argue that point until he looked at the terrified woman. Her hands were trembling, tears ran down her cheeks. "Fine."

He lifted a finger, and the officer nearest to the older woman walked over. "Can you take her to another room. I need to speak to her and have the EMTs check her out."

The moment the officer tried to take Aracely away, the older woman cried out and wouldn't leave without Ari. It took less than five minutes for Detective Westin to give in and allowed all three of them to wait in the front lounge area for EMTs.

"Pretty good, huh?" Aracely said once the police left them alone.

"I thought you were laying it on kind of thick," Ari said, with a smile.

"I don't know you, but it was Oscar-worthy," Lucas chimed in.

The older woman gave a flourished hand gesture with a bow. "Thank you. I couldn't leave you guys out there with them. I'm pretty sure that detective doesn't hate you."

"What?! Of course he does. It's damned exhausting arguing with him."

"He's not afraid of you. That's a good quality in an esposo," Aracely nodded sagely.

Ari cut the side-eye towards the older woman. "I'm not sure what 'esposo' means, but no. No good qualities in that man."

Lucas covered his laugh. Aracely giggled along with him.

"Ms. Aracely, we are going to have to agree to disagree on the matter of Detective Adam Westin. He doesn't like me, and I certainly don't like him."

"Whatever you say, mija."

The wind chime tone on Ari's cellphone indicated she had a new text message. She stared at Lucas after reading it and gave a grim smile.

It was time.

CHAPTER 24

It took another hour for the police to finish questioning the trio and to get Aracely all taken care of. There wasn't any kind of magic Ari could wield to move the process along faster, but when she got into her car, Tiffany proved why she was called the ultimate driving machine.

"When you sped away from the old folks home, I didn't think it was for tapioca." Lucas awkwardly chomped on the chewy balls of sweetness from his bubble tea.

Ari looked out into the HK-Chine shopping center walkway, then took another sip of her own strawberry-banana smoothie. She chewed some tapioca before answering. "This is where he said to meet him."

"Him? Leif?!"

"Shhhh." Ari looked at the other six people inside the smoothie shop, No one looked up. "What's wrong with you? Obviously, if we're playing cloak and dagger, something's wrong."

Lucas scooted his chair next to his cousin, then leaned in. "You think he found her?"

Ari shook her head before patting his hand. "I don't know. I hope so."

Before he could ask another question she couldn't answer, her phone chimed. She opened her text messages. Lucas leaned in to look over her shoulder. She couldn't blame him. She wanted to know already.

"Come on."

Lucas was out of his seat before she could get her purse over her shoulder. They both threw their drinks away before walking through the Asian grocery store. Ari read the label on a pack of ramen when a cold breeze drifted over her hand. Her head snapped up.

"I'm here. Don't look around." Leif said from behind her, then reached over her to grab a package of noodles.

"Why didn't you just come to the house? This is crazy," Ari whispered as she pretended to read the label.

"I'm pretty sure I'm being followed. At least I was."

An older couple pushed a basket down the aisle. Ari watched them from the corner of her eye, until they turned a corner. "Okay, well, tell me what's going on? Is she okay?"

"I only saw her once, but she was pretty out of it." He moved down the aisle behind Ari.

"Those damned drugs," Ari mumbled. "We gotta get her away from them."

"They're moving her tonight."

"What?" Her head whipped around. "That's not enough time."

"It's what we got. I'll text you when and where when I find out."

"I've been looking all over for you." Lucas grabbed Leif by the shoulders. "You find her? Is she okay?" He took a long breath, then asked, "Is she still alive?"

"She is. For now. I gotta go, Ari will fill you in." He walked past her, then abruptly stopped. Leaving them shoulder to shoulder. His fingers intertwined with hers, then squeezed.

He put more passion and tenderness in that single touch than she'd felt in a really long time. And just like that he was gone.

"She's still alive. What else did he say?"

She pulled out her phone. "I'll tell you on the way."

They needed a little backup.

WHAT IS GOING on with him? "Buster, I need you." Ari paced around her living room.

"Ari, I can't," Buster said.

"You can't or you won't?" Ari yelled, but then took a deep breath to get it together. "Talk to me Buster, please." Only a groan from the other end of the line, but nothing else. "You can't stay cooped up in that little apartment forever."

"You know how difficult it is this time of year," Buster said.

"I do know," Ari replied.

Then really thought about it. The streets were usually teeming with spirits. In all honesty, it was pretty damned tame in the city. Something was going on.

"This is a matter of life and death," Ari pleaded.

"I wish I could, but the answer's, no," Buster said sternly.

Ari didn't detect any sign of sympathy or empathy. She'd never known Buster to not care, especially about someone he knew. Before she could stop herself, the words fell out of her mouth.

"Benedict Homer Calaveras, one day you'll need someone's help and you better pray I'm not the only person around," she growled the last, then hit the off button.

"Ari, is everything okay?"

Ari almost didn't recognize her. One long leg peaked out of a red and black flamenco dancer costume. A ruby stone in a silver head-dress? A costume?

"Oh, my goddess. It's Halloween. I'm so sorry."

"It's okay. Buster took me last week." The black cloak fluttered as she whipped it around her shoulders.

"Buster?" After Nyah nodded, Ari said, "That was nice of him. So where are you off to tonight?"

"I made a few friends. I believe we are doing something called a stroll." Nyah shrugged a shoulder.

Where had she been that she missed Nyah making friends? When did that happen? "Oh, that's great. Strolls are fun. Be careful, it's always crazy on Halloween."

Nyah waved her phone and pepper spray from her small bag. "I'll be okay." She reached out and touched Ari's hand. "Whatever it is. It tis always darkest before the dawn. My father always said that to the village. It was always before war, but a good saying even now, yes?"

The stones in Ari's protection bracelet didn't activate, but instead warmed her entire wrist. That hadn't happened before. She slid her hand out of Nyah's before saying, "Yes. It's a good saying. Have fun tonight." At least one of them should.

Ari grabbed her messenger bag and looked over the potion rack near the kitchen.

Lucas came in from the balcony. "I still don't like her. Always wanting to touch people." He shivered. "Gives me the creeps every time."

"She's not that bad."

She placed a few bottles into the bag. Then sniffed a dried spring of lavender and sage and stuffed a few into her bag as well.

"You know I'm telling the truth," Lucas said with his arms folded.

He was, but Ari wasn't going to tell him that. Instead, she rolled her eyes. "Come on." She opened the door.

"Where are we going?" He grabbed his jacket off the back of the sofa.

"Get some backup."

CHAPTER 25

The music was so loud, the bass rattled Ari's back teeth. It had been a long time since she worked a Halloween and now, she remembered why. Not only was it a sacred witch holiday, it was her favorite holiday, period.

The bouncer dressed in his normal all black, waved her in with a two-fang smile. She and Lucas made their way through the throngs of vampires, dressed in their finest, along with werewolves, fairies and superheroes. For the first time in a long time, Ari was out of place in the goth bar.

Ari waved her hand in front of her cousin's face. "Hey."

Lucas looked around her hand. "I'll be fine. Do what you need to do." He swirled his finger and the waitress with the bat wings tripped forward, exposing the nice curve of her butt atop fish net thigh highs.

She fought her way through the crowd, but had to pause at the pointy hatted sexy witch. The girl sneered as she pushed Ari out of her way. Which was no easy task in her six-inch, 'fuck me' heels. One of Ari's fingers lit with a dime sized flame, then flicked it as if thumping a bug. The frilly lace of the witch's micro mini dress caught fire instantly. The netting tulle seemed to go up in seconds.

The fake witch hopped around patting out the flame. The crowd parted like the Red Sea and Ari walked up to the bar counter and grabbed the pitcher of beer left behind in the melee.

Just as she tossed the beer to put of the fire, an unnatural wind blasted through the bar and the girl's stitch-of-a-costume fell apart at the seams. Served her right for dressing like a skanky witch. The girl stormed out with running mascara, wild hair, and a burned up and soaking wet dress. She might have tossed most of the beer in the fake witch's face and only partly on the fire. Accidents happen.

Ari looked around for Lucas. With a slight nod in his direction, her cousin disappeared back into the crowd of Halloween revelers.

"What the hell?" Bull rushed from the back with the extinguisher in his hands.

"It's over. I put her out," Ari said with an angelic smile as she walked behind the bar.

"What are you doing here?" Bull eyed her suspiciously.

"Bull, aren't you happy to see me?" She batted her lashes. Maybe one time too many.

"Cut the bullshit. What you want?"

Ari put her hands on her hips. "Why would you say such a thing?"

"You never come here on Halloween. Whatever you want the answer's no."

Bull walked away, and pointed at the bat-waitress. "Whatchu need?" She told him and he grabbed long necks from the cooler.

Ari followed him. "It's life or death."

"Really? Now we're getting somewhere. Whose?" Bull said to her, then pointed at the Nosferatu at the bar with his long fingernail up.

"My cousin. I need..." She jumped in front of him. "Look, I wouldn't be here if I wasn't desperate."

"How much?" Bull folded his arms.

Ari looked confused. "What?"

"You need money, right? She in jail?"

"No, no. Nothing like that. I want..." She looked up as a young man carrying a pallet of glasses turned the corner. "I need him."

Ari pointed at Jacque.

Crash. Glass went everywhere. Jacque stood staring at her, then looked behind him. "Were you… you talking about me?"

"God dammit, boy. What the hell?" Bull grabbed a pan and broom.

"Yes. Come out of the glass, Jacque." Ari held her hand out to him.

Jacque didn't seem to hear his boss cursing him to high heaven, he kept staring at her. Then he reached for her hand, stepping out of the shards of glass.

"If he's going to be this much of a pain. Take him. It's his last night anyway," Bull said as he pushed past them.

"What? You're quitting?"

He looked away and tightened his lips.

"Okay, we'll talk about that later. Come with me." Ari pulled his hand, not giving him any choice and walked him outside.

"You want my help?" Jacque said after Ari explained the situation. He touched his chest as he emphasized the word *my*.

"Of course, why wouldn't I?" Ari grabbed his hands.

"No one has ever wanted anything from me, except to get away. My mother only tolerates me because I'm her only child." He shook his head in disbelief.

"Jacque, look at me." When he did, she continued. "You're my friend and you might not believe this, but I don't have a lot of those. One, I don't want you to go. And two, I need to save my cousin from some crazy ass witches. So, you with me or what?"

"If you want me, I'm yours."

Then he did something, Ari had rarely seen him do in all the time she'd known him. Smiled. She opened her arms and he seemed to fall into them with a heavy thunk. With him, she'd found that any sort of touch was important, simply because no one ever had. It must have been a difficult growing up with witches all fearing he would steal their power.

"No, no, no," Lucas said from a few feet away.

Jacque bristled in her arms before they pulled apart. She snatched his hand and held it when he tried to pull away.

"I can... can move," Jacque stammered out.

"You can stand right here," Ari whispered back.

"We don't need him, Ari." Still not coming any closer.

"We do and he's not going to hurt you. Will you come over here? I am not yelling out this conversation."

Her cousin stubbornly only took three steps closer. "Maybe, try Buster again."

"We're out of time. Leif sent me the address. We go now if we're saving Rum."

Lucas stared at her shaking her head. "This is a bad idea."

"Duly noted," Ari said, then walked towards her car.

"It might be better if I take my bike. Confined spaces." Jacque said as he looked over her car.

"I'll text you the address."

"You can just tell me. I have a great memory. I'll be there."

Ari told him, then jumped into the car.

"He ain't gonna show," Lucas said, shaking his head.

"Jacque isn't like that. He'll show."

She prayed to the goddess above that he showed. Lucas may not realize it, but they were going to be outgunned at this rescue party. If Jacque didn't show, they were all dead.

CHAPTER 26

The address led Ari and Lucas to a warehouse business park. Lucas and Ari watched the property from behind a row of boxwoods and crepe myrtles from across the street. Rows and rows of beige and brown stone buildings with large bay doors, loading ramps and docks. There was nothing that screamed, 'Witch Torture Center'. It all looked so mundane.

"Is this where you escaped from?" Ari kept looking forward. In her peripheral, she could see her cousin shake his head.

"None of this looks familiar." The wind picked up around them.

Ari touched his hand. "That won't help us now. I need you focused."

They were both silent for a few minutes. "They did this to suppress her powers. Look around, it's all concrete and steel."

Behind them, footsteps walked along the gravel path. They both whirled around, with powers on. Both of Ari's hands were wrapped in a bright orange blaze. Lucas held his hands low, but dirt and small rocks swirled in a small tornado at his feet.

"Whoa, whoa," Jacque said with both hands out. "No need for that."

"How the hell did you find us?" Lucas shook out his hands and the baby tornadoes died.

"I can feel magical energy. Psychic, mental, or physical, even crystals if they're powerful enough." Jacque moved next to Ari.

Ari was actually really impressed. There's really no info on what all a psyphon could do. Maybe because most witches were afraid of them.

"That's so cool," Ari said.

At the same time Lucas said, "Of course you can."

"Don't pay him any mind." Ari pulled him closer to her. "Can you tell if they're in the building? If they are, then we got here too late."

"I don't know. I've never tried from this far away before." Jacque eased out from behind the crepe myrtle.

With his eyes closed, Jacque waved his outstretched hand the expanse of the property. His hand whipped back to the middle of the complex and his eyes snapped open.

"Fou… found them. But—"

"But? But what?" Lucas said when he and Ari surrounded Jacque. "Is she? Can you tell if my sister's alive?"

"Yes. Tha… tha." Jacque took a deep breath, then tried again. "That's not the problem."

"Slow down and tell us what they did," Ari said as she put a hand on his arm.

He gave her a grateful smile, before explaining. "There are seven magical signatures. One is really faint."

"We can take them," Lucas said. "I know we can."

"That's not the problem." Jacque shook his head. "They are the center of a pentagram of dark energy."

"Goddess above." Ari stared at the warehouses. "They really don't want anyone getting inside of there."

This type of ward used the blood of all those inside to create a security force field around the large building. Ari had only heard about the ward, but never actually seen it.

"No, they don't want anyone in the coven to know what they are doing to their own people," Lucas said softly. "We have to get her out of there. No matter what, Ari. We can't… I can't. She got me out. I have to get her out."

"We will." Ari rubbed his arm.

His aura swirled through every color of the rainbow. Lucas's emotions ranged from murderous, being a savior, self-inflicted pain, fear, rage, and rescuing his sister all rolled into one.

"I know this is difficult," Ari said to Lucas. "But think. Did anyone, your mom maybe, ever say how to deactivate the ward?"

Lucas looked past her in thought. "I remember Mom saying we didn't use it because it took too much magic to hold the ward. Unlike others, this one constantly draws from the individual's magic residing within the ward."

"They are weakened, somewhat. That's good. What else?" Ari urged him on.

"Um, the energy will fry us if we try to cross it. I remember that," Lucas said.

Jacque added softly. "I can divert the energy."

"What part of fry don't you understand?" Lucas said.

"Wait, Lucas. He may have something. If he can, then the ward goes down right?"

Lucas nodded. "Sure, but he'll be dead."

"How's the energy contained? It can't just be the blood moving that much power around."

"Oh, yeah. They got these beach ball sized quartz crystal clusters they have to use."

A smile slid across Jacque's face. "I know how we're getting in."

THE BLOOD ENERGY pulsed sharply in front of Ari. That much power made the hair on the back of her neck stand on end. The scent of this much blood reminded her of a dark time in her life. She knew she wasn't that girl anymore, but the urge to kill still lingered deep inside her. That was her burden to bear, and this was partly her fault. She would endure this and more to help her cousin.

With angry protest, Lucas agreed to hide until the ward was

down and the fight began.

"I'm sure I stood here long enough that they know I'm here. Let's get this party started," Ari said to Jacque. "If I didn't say it before, thank you. I know you didn't have to come."

He looked up at her with a smile. "Now, remember what I said."

"I understand. Just try not to blow us up if it comes to that."

He nodded with a smile that could have rivaled the Cheshire cat. "I'll do my best." He then turned back, held his hands out like he was warming them by the fire.

Ari couldn't see it but she could feel it the moment he began to withdraw the magic, the ward wavered. She was sure everyone inside felt it as well. She closed her eyes and stilled her nerves for whatever was about to happen. A pulse of energy whipped out and Ari stumbled.

"Sorry. So much... magic," Jacque stammered out through grunts.

Ari righted herself, then pulled her hand back when she nearly touched him. "You okay?"

He gave a tight nod. "Here they come."

A cool breeze flowed over her hands and she knew it was Lucas showing his support or he wanted in on the fight. She waved her hand behind just as the three male witches in jeans and t-shirts burst out the door, then laughed. The ward was still up but barely.

"What do you want?" The brawny, dark haired - fair skinned man asked after laughing.

Ari looked directly at the men as she whispered to Jacque. "How close?"

"Almost. Be ready." He then slipped his hand under the hem of her pants around her ankle.

Somehow Ari believed Jacque when he revealed that he could transfer the magic to someone else if done quickly.

"I believe you have my cousin in there. Would you be so kind as to bring her out?"

"Look," the brawny guy answered, "This is private property. You can't come in for any reason. Now, go home."

A tingling sensation ran up Ari's leg. Everything in her tightened up. She wasn't sure her body could contain this much magic.

"Take deep breaths," Jacque whispered. "And get ready."

"Please, I don't want to hurt you," Ari said.

"You hear that. Let's show her what hurt really is," Brawny said. He cracked his neck and flexed his arms before nicking his hand with a small knife. They all had blood on their hands before moving towards Ari.

She still hadn't powered up, the magic filled every corner of her body. It was acupuncture needles prickling her entire body. Jacque removed his hand and slumped on the ground. Then all the magic that held the ward up was gone. A lot of it was inside her.

Power surged out of her so swiftly, it frightened her. A bright orange enveloped her hands and blasted from her fingertips before she even realized what had happened. Instead of small balls of fires, it was as if a blowtorch blasted from each finger, not just the palm of her hand.

The two men on the side of Brawny began to scream, holding their faces. Goddess, with that much fire power she could have killed them. Brawny wasn't deterred by his fallen comrades and came at her full force. Ari was so distraught about the men she'd nearly killed; she hadn't noticed the knife until it hit her in the arm.

"Ari!" Lucas called out from behind her.

Fear kept her from using the fire magic burning to get out. Knives formed in Brawny's hand as he barreled down on her. All the logical things ran through her mind: like she should fight back, like he was going to kill her, like she'd rather die with honor.

There wasn't much blood, but she cradled the spot where the knife hit none-the-less. She cringed and braced for what would surely be a death blow. A stiff breeze rocked her. Metal clanged on the ground like raindrops. An arm slid around her waist pulling her up against a smaller frame.

"No," Jacque whispered. "Not today."

She opened her eyes to a spray of knives on the ground and Brawny laid at her feet.

"What were you going to do, just let him kill you?" Lucas said hotly.

Ari couldn't answer him truthfully, so she said nothing. She looked at the hand around her waist, then into big blue eyes. "I'm okay." She tapped his hand and he released her.

"Is he?" Ari nodded towards Brawny.

"Yes. I'm sorry. He was going to kill you. I could see it in his eyes," Jacque said clear and without stuttering.

"I understand."

"Hey, Jacque. What you did for Ari? Can you…" Lucas tilted his head.

Ari didn't say anything to ruin this monumental occasion. But she was positive her cousin had never once called Jacque by his name. She watched them both.

"Sure. Give me your arm."

Lucas stretched out his arm. "Will it hurt?"

Jacque looked at Ari. "I don't know. You'll have to ask Ari. She was the first person I'd ever performed it on." He grabbed Lucas just below the elbow, before he could snatch his arm back.

The entire transfer took less than a minute. Lucas flexed his fingers. Seconds later, smoke rose from where eight little divots had formed in the side of the building.

"Demons below, this is awesome." Lucas waved his hand around.

Ari and Jacque ducked, both yelling, "Whoa!"

"It's only temp… temporary. At least, I think it is. We might want to hurry," Jacque said.

"Can we try not to kill anyone else?" Ari held up her hand when Jacque opened his mouth. "I know it was unintentional. I would like my mother not to rain blood justice down on us, that's all." *It was already going to be bad enough as is.*

"Sure, whatever you say," Lucas said, before he walked inside.

"That… that didn't sound good," Jacque said.

Ari shook her head. "No, that didn't."

She knew her cousin, and that definitely sounded like he would kill whoever got in his way.

"Come on. Before he gets himself hurt and then we'll have to save him too."

CHAPTER 27

The lack of more security surprised Ari. Jacque guided them through the maze of narrow hallways with faded motivational slogans of cats hanging by their paws and footprints in the sand, and empty dust covered cubicles. This place looked like it hadn't been occupied in many years.

They'd all turned off their phones and gone silent, using only hand gestures to communicate with each other. Jacque snapped his fist in the air and Lucas and Ari stopped in their tracks.

This was it. Whoever was on the other side of the door, knew they were inside the building. It would have made sense to run, but the Black Blood coven never ran from a fight. At least, that's what her mother used to drill into everyone.

Jacque held up four fingers. Then moved to open the door. He didn't get a chance. Gale force winds blasted the door off its hinges.

Ari could only stare at her cousin.

"What? They already know we're here," Lucas said, as he stepped inside. "Might as well make an entrance."

There was nothing she could say or do. What was done was done, all they could do now was save her cousin. Hopefully, without killing anyone.

"Lucas, wait." Ari stepped into complete darkness and immediately grabbed Jacque's hand. *Damn it.* "Are they still here?" she whispered.

"Yes, we are," a familiar female voice answered.

Ari released Jacque's hand and held both of hers out and let her power flow through her. An orange blaze erupted from her hands straight into the air. She counted to three and tightened her will to control the power. It immediately stopped imitating a volcano eruption and began to swirl into small beach ball sized suns. Both flaming orbs floated upward.

The room lit up like it was the middle of the day. Lucas stood to her far right and Jacque had moved along the wall to her left. She knew Leif would be there. She was saddened, but not surprised to see her aunt.

Ari gasped through splayed fingers. Her eyes focused on Rum, who hung by a metal chain like a slab of meat. "Luca Bee."

"How could you? That's your daughter!" Lucas pointed up towards the center of the room.

"Children should do as they're told." Tatum didn't even look up. "This would have never happened if you would have just given the high priestess what she'd asked for. Not staying loyal to her." Tatum looked directly at Ari then.

"Mom!"

Lucas lifted his hand in her direction. The fast-moving air began to ruffle everyone's clothes. Ella Grace moved in front of Tatum, but the older woman put her hand on the girl's shoulder. Tatum whispered something, the girl looked up towards Rum, then Ari, then nodded before easing away.

"Son, you are no match for me so just drop the act. There's still a spot for you in our coven. Just tell us where she hid the witch and his grimoire."

"After what you've done? To your own children." Lucas cringed like someone had squeezed his heart. "Ari, I can't keep my word."

The winds picked up, whirling around the room. Every rock, pebble, dirt, and speck of dust was carried along for the ride.

"Release her. Let her down, now."

"You want her? Get her yourself." Tatum folded her arms and waited.

Couldn't he see she was baiting him? Parents always had a way of laying on a nerve and knowing just how you will react.

Lucas whipped his hand out in a slash. Ari figured it out, he was trying to cut through the chain with his wind magic. His magic was ineffective against the wards surrounding it.

"Lucas," Ari said as she watched Ella Grace.

Ella Grace smiled as she walked along the wall.

"Lucas, stop it!"

He couldn't hear her or didn't want to. Ari ran towards him, but something whistled past her ear. A barrage of bright pink-filled darts flew in Lucas' direction. He whipped up his hand and the darts scattered around the room.

Leif held his hands out as the magic dampeners came in his direction. He sent out bursts of cold, freezing the darts mid-air and they all fell to the floor. Ella Grace's smile faltered when Tatum clasped her neck and stumbled backward.

"Mistress!" Ella Grace ran to Tatum's motionless body.

Ella Grace lowered Tatum's hand from her neck. The empty dart hung limply. She gingerly pulled it out, then glared at Ari, then Lucas. "You won't get away with this."

The young woman grabbed two vials and slammed them on the ground. The mixture released a bright white flash and a loud bang. A dark gray smoke filled the back half of the room. Ari ran towards the thinning smoke. Like a magician, all three of them were gone.

"Ari!" Jacque ran to the body sprawled out.

In all the ruckus, they hadn't realized that Lucas went down as well.

"I don't see a dart?" Jacque said as he touched the man's arms and legs.

"Let's turn him over."

Both sets of hands gently turned him and there it was, dangling from his neck.

"What is that stuff?" Pointing towards the small amount of neon pink liquid still in the vial.

"Don't touch it." Ari used the bottom of her shirt to extract the needle from Lucas' neck. "It's fucking poison. That's what it is."

"Will it kill him?"

Ari shook her head. "No, but he won't be able to use his magic for a few hours."

"Can I keep it?"

Ari stared him like he had sprouted two heads. "Why? This is horrible stuff."

"I… I want to study it. See what it's made of. May… maybe find an antidote?"

He didn't sound too sure about the last part. Ari eyed him a bit longer.

"If you don't think," Jacque began.

"No, no. I just didn't realize you were into science, that's all. If you could find a way to make sure this doesn't happen again. Great. My bag's at the door. Could you get it for me?"

He grabbed it and she wrapped the dart in a napkin and placed it inside.

"If you can lower the ward, I can get her down."

Jacque's skill at lowering wards was impressive. Witches followed so many of the old ways and had so many prejudices, they had no idea how amazing psyphons really were.

Ari looked at the two bodies on the floor and sighed. Her place was truly becoming a motel.

CHAPTER 28

The twins took up her entire queen-sized bed. Although, Rum was nothing more than skin and bones. It was hard to believe her mother and Aunt Tatum could stoop to that level.

"Are they okay?" Jacque asked from the couch.

Ari sat down in the armchair. "Yeah, they'll probably sleep till morning." She flexed her fingers. It took about two hours, but all of the extra magic had dissipated.

"Is it all gone?"

She nodded. "Are you okay? It seemed to take a lot out of you."

"For a while, I was happy. I was able to help you. I never thought my powers were good for anything but taking. I don't know, it felt good. You know?"

She did know. It was why she kept volunteering and reading tarot, and on occasion, the rescue mission.

"You have a nice place," Jacque said.

The place was a mess. Dishes were dirty, laundry was still in the basket unfolded from last week. And let's not even talk about her work bench. Ari smiled and said, "Thanks."

"Do you live by yourself?"

"No, I have a roomie. It's a temporary situation. Helping out a... a guy I know."

Nyah must be still out with her new friends. In a way, she was kind of jealous. This was her favorite holiday, but she didn't get to do any of the fun witch things.

"Your family, huh?" Jacque lowered his head in a shy smile.

"Yep. That's the sorta crazy I come from."

"Much like mine. Except with my mom, everyone needed to be dressed to the nines at all times. Designer everything. If she saw me right now." He looked down at his filthy tee and ran his hands over the dirt on his jeans, then smiled. "She would probably have a heart-attack. It's all about appearances with her."

"I had a thing for shoes for a while, but they kept getting ruined. It's hard to run in stilettos, let me tell you." The both laughed at that

Remy's image flickered in. "Remy?"

Jacque looked around. "Is your place haunted?"

Ari watched the spot where Remy just stood. "Why would you ask that?"

"I feel..."

Remy appeared, his mouth opened and shut like he was saying something, but there was no sound.

"That." Jacque said moving to where Remy stood, but looking right through him. "You have a ghost."

"I know," she said to Jacque but kept her eyes on Remy. "What is it Remy? What's happening?"

He pointed towards her phone, then flickered out. "Remy!"

"Ari, what is it?" Jacque asked.

Ari fumbled with her phone. "I don't know." She slid her finger over the phone and finally the screen lit up.

Rows and rows of missed call and text notifications scrolled along the screen. She checked the two text messages first. They were from Buster. Nothing much, he just apologized.

The phone calls were a different story. She could hear people screaming in the background, windows breaking. She pulled the phone away from her ear.

"I gotta go."

Ari stumbled around with her phone in her hand, then she grabbed her bag and shoes, but didn't put them on.

Jacque grabbed her arms to stop her from going out the door. "What's going on?"

She snatched away from him. "I have to go. My friend's in trouble," she said through tears.

"Ari, do you have your keys?"

She patted her pockets and looked around in a circle.

"Okay, I'll get your keys. You put your shoes on."

Ari nodded and dropped the shoes right where she stood and slid her feet into the tennis shoes without untying them. Jacque reached into a bowl on the side table next to her. The keys jingled in his hand.

"I'll drive," Jacque said. "Just tell me where we're going."

The phone vibrated in her hand. "Hello, Buster, Buster, you okay?"

"Not, Buster. What going on?" Leif's rich voice came through the line.

"I don't know. We're going to check on him now."

"I'll meet you there, what's the address?"

It took her a minute to collect her thoughts. She wanted to argue about him blowing his cover, but in the end, she gave him the address because she just wanted him there.

Ari slammed the door, not even sure if she locked it as they raced to Buster's place.

CHAPTER 29

The ride from mid-town to Buster's didn't take long. But Ari could feel that something had changed. It was all around her the moment she walked out of her building. A sad sense of foreboding sat on her heart and she couldn't shake it.

Buster's business and home, Bust-A-Sud Washateria, wasn't in the best neighborhood, but kids were still dressed up in their scary best. Jack-O-Lanterns were bright and some yards, and even a few balconies in the apartment complexes, were decorated. This lifted the dread looming over her a bit. Maybe because she just witnessed a level of darkness in her family she never thought she'd see. And for what? Haviland? His grimoire?

No.

Erissa wanted power. All of this was about gaining his power. A level of magic no one had seen in more than 500 years. Her mother wasn't going to let anything, or anyone, get in her way. Including family.

The car slowed down. "What the?"

Ari looked up and couldn't quite grasp what she was seeing. The broken windows and doors were a new look. What she didn't expect was the line of dirt-covered, and somewhat meaty skeletons in front of the building.

Jacque and Ari stood next to Tiffany and watched the unmoving creatures. A family walked down the sidewalk, past the dead. They pointed and laughed at what they must have thought were Halloween decorations.

Remy appeared before her arms waving wildly.

"What are you saying?"

She still couldn't hear him, then he pointed upstairs, before disappearing.

"Remy?"

"We gotta get inside," Ari said as she crossed the street.

"I don't think they are just going to let us in."

"We can try," Ari whispered.

She walked towards the doors that hung askew off its hinges. The moment she tried to squeeze by, the dead came to life. They closed ranks and blocked the opening. Each one turned their heads in a mechanical, and synchronized way. An unnerving sense of dread swamped Ari as they focused their fathomless dark eye sockets directly on her.

When they attempted to breach the doors again a boney set of fingers wrapped around her throat. She'd glanced in Jacque's direction just in time to see him being tossed across the street by a bigger, meatier skeleton. Even through the blood rushing to her ears, she heard the impact. Tiffany had taken another one for the team.

Its skeletal fingers tightened around her neck, barely a breath squeaked out with each kick. Black spots appeared and disappeared before her eyes. She always thought death would come at the hands of a great witch or maybe even old age. Not a pack of bones.

She closed her eyes, then a cold, biting wind cut through her. The ground didn't give an inch when she landed.

"You okay?"

She blinked to see a pair of beautiful, clear blue eyes staring down at her. She wanted to kiss him. She wanted to do a lot of things in that moment, but she needed to get inside. Before Ari could think better of it, she lifted up, and pulled him in closer.

Pressing her lips against his with a ferocity that could only happen when you were ecstatic to see someone and glad that you were alive. The kiss was brief, but she got her point across.

"Thanks. Now, help me up." She extended her hand and he snatched her up.

She looked at the row of frozen broken bones. "Nice work," Ari said with a smile.

"I try."

"Hey, Jacque," she looked back, "you okay?"

Jacque nodded and limped across the street. "Yeah, I might need to get some armor if I'm gonna hang with you."

"Not a bad idea. Come on."

The washers and dryers were covered in blood. Bodies of men, women, and children were sprawled out on the floor covered in even more blood. Ari couldn't help them, but she could probably save her friend. A surge of urgency rose in her and she burst through the door that led up to Buster's apartment.

THE WARDS on Buster's apartment were down. Ari had never known of a time where the protection wasn't in place. She pushed the half-opened door wider and heard a melodic chant inside.

"Buster? You home?" *If he wasn't, someone was inside.*

She walked past the small anti-room and pushed aside the beaded curtain. "I'm so sorry." Ari moved to back out, bumping into Leif behind her.

"Help. Me."

The words were so faint, they were almost washed away by the swoosh of the beads. Ari turned and really looked at the woman writhing atop Buster's still form. At first glance, it seemed like she had walked in on an intimate moment.

Then a few things struck her odd: One - Buster did not seem like a willing participant. Two - she'd seen that dress before. Three - the room looked like a war-zone. Overturned and broken furniture, tarot cards all over the floor. Buster would never leave his place like that.

"Nyah?" Ari moved further into the room stepping over the broken leg of a chair. "Is that you?"

The chant stopped and the body stopped moving. "Go away, Aria. This does not concern you."

The figure didn't turn around, but she didn't have to. She'd heard that voice and looked at that wavy blonde hair for a while.

"Nyah? What are you doing to him?" Ari walked towards the two.

Leif and Jacque's step were soft, but she heard them walk into the room behind her. Nyah whipped around baring teeth with a growl as she thrust her hand out. An arc of magic cut through the room. Ari instinctually protected her face and her shield activated. The force of the magic pushed her backwards. Her tennis shoes couldn't get any traction and she slid back along the flooring for at least three feet.

Leif put up an ice shield and when the magic made contact, it nearly split in two. Jacque held his hands out like a baseball catcher, and he absorbed it. He gave a wicked smile, that screamed, *gotta do better than that.*

Ari wasn't exactly sure what she was seeing. White and black makeup contoured the young woman's previously beautiful face creating a skull facade.

"Interesting friends you have." Nyah's gaze lingered over Jacque a little too long. "I have a friend, as well. He's been most helpful." Nyah held her hand out. "Remy."

Remy appeared exactly at Nyah's fingertips. "Yes, mistress."

"What have you done to him?" Blue flames engulfed Ari's hands and she took a step forward.

"Temper, temper. You wouldn't want to pass out." Nyah lowered herself and touched Buster's face. It was the exact skull makeup she had on. "Now, Buster will die if you choose to chase me. Or I can give you Remy as a sign of good faith. He might even help you get this carcass to the hospital. Although, I don't think there is much hope for him." She stood up and kicked Buster's unmoving body. "Your choice."

"I helped you. Took you into my home. Taught you how to function. Buster and I both did. How could you do this?" The room was suddenly flooded in a bright blue light.

Leif pressed a cool hand to her neck and another hand touched her shoulder. The blue light dimmed down.

"Such power. I would have loved to control you. But you resisted me at every turn." Nyah circled Ari.

Unwilling to allow the enemy at their back, they turned as one, following Nyah's path. "You don't have to do this. I can put Royal back. You can be with Havil—"

"Don't," Nyah cut in. "Even say his name."

"He loves you. He did…"

"Everything I told him to. Everyone thought because my legs didn't work, that I was useless. But my mind worked just fine. And with one touch." Nyah gave a devious smile.

"You won't get away with this," Ari said.

"Sweet child. I already have. You just haven't realized it yet." Nyah murmured a few words under her breath, before walking out the door.

Remy fell to his knees. Ari dropped down next to him.

"Cher, je suis désolé. Before I realized what she could do, she had all of us and we couldn't tell you a thing."

"I know. I know. This is not your fault." The tears streamed down her face. All she wanted to do was hold him and that wasn't possible.

Sirens blared outside. They weren't there for her, but it felt like it.

"Someone must have walked in on that bloodbath downstairs," Leif said.

"If… if we go down now, they'll think we did it. If we stay here, with Buster's body they'll think we're hiding."

"Remy, are you okay enough to check on what's going on out there?"

Remy disappeared before she finished asking. She moved to

Buster and lowered her head to his chest. Then touched his neck for a pulse. Faint, but still in the land of the living.

"Is he?"

"Still alive, but we gotta get him out of here." His aura was pretty much non-existent. She'd drained him of everything that made him… him.

Remy reappeared. Jacque looked in his direction, but Leif was completely unaware.

"There are no bodies. She took everyone," Remy said.

Ari told the boys what Remy said, then added, "Remy's going to take Buster to the hospital. We are walking out the front door. If the police ask, the party got a little bit rowdy."

"And the blood?" Leif asked.

"Fake. All fake." Ari looked at Remy. "Do it now, we're outta here."

Buster's body jerked and convulsed as Remy took control. Jacque and Leif gaped as the body sat straight up, all horror movie killer, Jason-style.

"That is incredibly creepy," Jacque said.

"It's going to get a helluva lot creepier," Ari said, as she helped Remy/Buster get steady on his legs.

"Buster was… is a necromancer. Now, Nyah is…"

"Malveillante garce," Remy supplied, then spat.

"Yes, that. But now she's an evil, powerful, necromancer bitch."

CHAPTER 30

It was hard to pretend to be happy and fun-lovin' with blood on your hands. They all opted to clean up a little bit before bursting into the washateria and current crime scene.

A police officer pointed a gun and called out, "Put your hands up."

The group had opened the *Employees Only* door laughing and talking loudly. Someone else blinded them with a flashlight.

Ari, Jacque, Leif, and Remy/Buster complied. Acting wasn't her thing, but to get out of this mess she would have to pull out an Oscar-worthy performance.

She lifted her arm to block the light. "Officer, could you please lower the light?"

It moved down a smidge, mostly from being directly in their eyes.

"What are you doing here? Are you the owner?" The same officer yelled out again.

"We were here for a party. It got a bit out of hand, as you can see." Ari waved around at the discarded clothes and broken dryer doors, half hanging open. "Can we put our hands down?"

"Yeah. We got a report of..."

"Let me guess. Dead bodies. Truthfully, we did have bodies here. All actors. Buster here, he's the owner. He knows how to throw a party. But after the window and doors got smashed, he asked everyone to leave."

The officer pulled out an iPad and he tapped the screen a few times, before speaking. "Sir, is that correct?"

Ari tapped Remy's hand. This was it, Remy had to sell it, or they were all going to go to jail.

He cleared his throat. "Yes, sir. This is me establishment."

It was weird to hear Remy speaking with Buster's Jamaican accent. He still had the Louisiana cadence, but this entire thing was just wrong. She had to get Buster back.

"Sir, could you come with me? Just need to answer some questions for my paperwork. And you might want to board everything up before you leave tonight."

This was the longest thirty minutes of her life. Only the officer taking care of the paperwork stayed. Ari could hear snippets of the calls that were coming in before the policemen began to race off.

In the distance, sirens were constantly going off. Smoke was thick in the air and orange glows were getting brighter all around them. Then the last officer got something called a ten-thirty-four and he sped out with lights flashing and sirens blaring.

"What the hell is going on?"

"This." Leif held the phone out and they all gathered around.

People in back-closing hospital gowns or 'johnnies' as Leise always called them, walked around tearing down street signs and overturning cars. Fires all over town. It was hard to imagine, but this was real.

"We gotta get Remy to the hospital and we're gonna need some more help." *And lots of it.*

STUNT DRIVING IS A LEARNED SKILL. Not hitting the living dead as they wander the streets during a pseudo-apocalypse takes talent. Ari hit the brakes hard after driving 70mph around downed power lines and burning buildings, people on fire, and the destructive dead. Ari's grip would be forever etched into the steering wheel.

"You all okay?" Ari's heart-rate hadn't come down.

She looked in the rearview mirror and saw that neither Jacque nor Leif had released the "oh, shit" bar.

"Guys, I think we better get inside," she said still looking out the rearview.

Jacque and Leif turned to look out the back window and saw the wave of stumbling hospital-johnnie-wearing people coming their way. Ari was already at the door of the White Cauldron when it swung open.

"Thank goddess," Ari said from the safety of a warded building. "Elizabeth, you..."

"Here?" Elizabeth finished for her with a smile. "I'm always here."

The door slammed once Jacque and Leif ran inside.

"Won't they be able to get inside?" Jacque said fumbling his words. Not asking anyone in particular.

"We've had a series of magic induced things happen here. We are well warded against most. Ari, the others are upstairs in the training room."

"Everyone?"

"Yes, when all of this started, they came here," Elizabeth said.

"Ms. Ari! Ms. Ari! I knew that was you," Oriana yelled from the back of the store.

A trail of adults and teens stepped off the back staircase. Drew and Oriana rushed across the store to hug Ari.

"It's the fucking zombie apocalypse," Oriana said excitedly.

"Language, young lady," a female voice said from the crowd.

"Yes, ma'am," Oriana said as she rolled her eyes.

The young girl pulled Ari further away from the parental units in the library, then looked around before speaking again. "It is freaking crazy though, right?"

"The moment the people in the hospital walked out, mom and dad jumped in the car to get here," Drew said, as she looked around. "Who are the guys?"

Ari couldn't help the smile that formed. "Those are my friends."

"Your boy... friends," Oriana sing-songed.

Ari tried to shhh them. Which just made them burst out into more fits of giggles. The ward lit the inside of the store with a bright electric blue light. A man with his hospital gown on backwards kept bumping into it. To the casual observer, he looked like a mime with his hands pressing against nothing because the actual window was about six-feet away from him.

"Oh, my." Elizabeth moved closer to the bay window.

Ari looked and when the girls' eyes went wide, she'd tried to cover their eyes, but they kept looking around her fingers to see the half-naked man. "Girls, go back to the library." Ari blocked their view with her body.

"Awww," Oriana and Drew said in unison.

Ari followed Elizabeth to the window, then lifted a brow when she was close enough to see the man in all his glory. "He has nothing to be ashamed of."

"Ari, I'm right here," Leif chimed in.

"Just making an observation," Ari called from over her shoulder.

"You are correct Ari, but that's not why I came over here." Elizabeth pointed towards his face. "Look at his eyes. They're dilated."

"And?"

"He's possessed. Now, that one." Elizabeth pointed. "Oh, he's dead."

A dirt covered skeleton with tattered and loose hanging clothes meandered by. It looked like a strong wind could knock it to pieces.

"It would help if we knew what kind of magic or even the spell, if they used one. I've just never seen so many controlled at once," Elizabeth spoke as she walked to the library in the back of the store.

An older, stocky man stepped away from the small crowd of witches. "Do we even know who's behind this?" Signet looked in everyone's direction.

When no one answered, the witches in the room started throwing out all kinds of suggestions.

Ari turned away from them and looked out the window and watched all the innocent victims walk by. She'd fucked up. Bad. Her city was burning to the ground and she had to make this right. Luscious and Michael could be out there stumbling around killing people, burning the city. Hell, they might get killed.

With her back to the room full of witches, Ari said, “I know who’s doing this.”

The room went quiet and she turned to face them. “I know who’s controlling all of these people. Her name is Nyah and she’s a 400-year-old witch that has stolen my friend’s necromancy power.”

Signet crossed his arms over his chest. Ari waited for judgment and accusations. This man had disliked her from the very start and tried to bar anyone in the White Cauldron witch group from talking to her. Later, they found out it was because his only son chose dark magic and broke with the family. Over the last few months, their relationship had progressed to speaking terms.

"How can we beat her?" Signet asked calmly.

Ari had to stop her mouth from flying open when he didn't bombard her with insults as per his usual reaction to evil and her.

Elizabeth spoke first. “I don’t know how to fight her kind of magic. It would take too long to search through the books to find anything close to the kind of magic she's using. I mean, I know something that might prevent possession.”

After regaining her composure, Ari chimed in. “That’s good. If a few of you spread out, protect the doctors, and set some wards at the hospital - that would be great. And…" she looked around the room, "Oriana?"

The young girl took a few steps from the back of the crowd. "Yes, ma'am."

"Can you work an illusion over the hospital? Is that too big?" Ari asked with bated breath as the girl thought about it.

Oriana's illusions looked like something out of the special effects team at Dreamworks. Although they looked realistic, a person could still walk through them. If the wards held, they should be able to save a lot of people.

"I think I can," Oriana said.

Ari prayed she could. For all their sakes.

“Wait, I can't teach the spell that fast,” Elizabeth said quickly.

Ari pulled Elizabeth to the side and whispered, "You have to take the potion. Only you can do this. We need the doctors alive. If I can beat her, maybe I can get Buster's power back."

Elizabeth looked around at the witches in the room, then at the dead outside.

"Oh, my goddess," Oriana said, looking at her cellphone. "The fucking… sorry, freaking zombies just took over Channel 26. They were everywhere, then they went off air."

Elizabeth reached for Ari's hands and squeezed them. "Okay, I'll get it ready."

Ari watched her go upstairs. "We think we have some kind of plan. Lizzie knows a protection spell against possession. I know who might know how to fight her, but you guys aren't going to like it. So, I'm going to have to do it myself."

Everyone started talking at once. "Hey, hey," Ari yelled above the ruckus. "This is my mess I have to clean it up."

"Why? Why is this just your mess?" Signet watched her carefully.

His tone was gentle, and he had never been that with her. Boy, they had come a long way. "She was my roommate and I didn't see how evil she was. This is on me."

"Do you have to do it alone?" Oriana looked around the room.

"She won't be. We'll be with her," Leif said, then looked at Jacque who nodded.

They had been so quiet she had forgotten that they were there. She mouthed, "Thank you," to them. Leif gave a slight bow and Jacque gave her that crooked shy smile.

"Ari," Remy called from in front of the bay window.

She rushed to the front door to move the warding stones that protected the building, giving him enough room to slide in. "What's happening out there?"

"It's bad. Whatever you're going to do, you better hurry. The hospital was in chaos. The coma patients were eating," Remy cringed. "Let's just say, things that weren't edible. You have to do something. The entire city will be at her mercy by morning."

"Buster?"

"They got him stabilized, but I don't think he has much time. She messed him up pretty bad."

Ari walked back to the stairs and yelled up, "Lizzie you ready? We gotta go."

Elizabeth came down in jeans and crisp button-down dress shirt with a faded, cracked black leather bomber jacket. As old as the woman was, that might actually be an original item. She held a messenger bag and doll in her hand, and a vial in the other.

"Well, what do you think?" Elizabeth twirled around.

There was stunned silence, then everyone whooped and complimented her.

"Okay, okay," Elizabeth spoke over them. "There are a few things we'll have to do to get the protection spell to work. If someone will load the ward stones, that would be great."

"I'll do it." Signet jumped up. "And you look great by the way."

"Me too," a tall thin man said.

"Thank you, Signet and Gerald. They're in the storage closet."

"You ready?" Ari whispered.

"Wait," Blossom, Oriana and Drew's mom, looked between the two ladies. "What are you going to do?"

"If it works it'll be a surprise. If it doesn't, then I'll use the doll."

The girls must have got it immediately, they covered their face as they gasped. Ari winked at them but didn't say a word. This was Elizabeth's moment.

It felt like that scene in Romeo and Juliet when Juliet drank the poison. But in this case, her friend would survive and become whole.

"Oh, I forgot. I made this for you." Ari handed her a quartz and copper ring. "I read that it's good to have something to ground you to this plane. Just in case."

Elizabeth slipped it on, then drank the liquid. "Mmm, at least it tastes good." She looked around at all the faces. After about a minute, she opened her mouth to say something, then she fell on all fours as an agonizing scream of pain came from her and thundered throughout the store.

She waved away every set of hands that tried to help her. When she said, "No!" The growl sounded more like a bear than a sweet-natured metaphysical store owner.

She contorted on the floor for what seemed like ten minutes, and they were all helpless to assist her.

"Help her." Oriana was in tears now. "Ari, what did you do?"

There were no words. She was sure this would work.

Did she kill another friend tonight?

CHAPTER 31

The city was crumbling under Nyah's living dead army, and for nearly an hour Ari didn't care. Elizabeth drank the potion to make her wholly human, with a real body. Not just an air spirit that existed within the confines of the brick and mortar building, like she had been since her death more than a hundred years ago.

It seemed like she would die another death at the hands of someone who supposedly cared about her. It took another thirty minutes, but the potion worked. Elizabeth looked like hell, but she could talk and walk. The girls and Signet helped her to the car, before he drove like a bat out of hell towards the medical center.

All of the witches decided to concentrate on one hospital and protect it. Oriana would use her illusion ability to make the space look empty and after the ward stones had been placed around the building, the adult witches could keep any stray zombies from entering.

There was no need to sneak into the cemetery. Ari drove past the crumpled metal in the streets. Gates normally kept people out. That didn't seem to be the case this time. This place had a stillness that was more eerie than anything. Upturned dirt revealed empty grave after empty grave. Headstones were knocked over. Even the doors to the property chapel were broken.

"This ain't right," Jacque whispered. Breaking the silence in the car. "Do you think she did this at every graveyard?"

Ari didn't say anything. She couldn't find the words. Leif didn't turn around as he answered the question.

"I'm sure she did." Leif spoke just above whisper.

She stopped the car in front of the O'Malley's mausoleum. At least, she thought it was the correct place. The building had been completely trashed. Ari could only guess that all of this destruction was Nyah's doing. A way of saying, she was never going back.

Glass cracked underfoot as she stepped through the gaping hole where the doors used to be. "Guys be careful. I think she broke every window in here."

She stopped short when she made it to the crypt where she'd stashed Haviland's body. It was completely destroyed. She picked up a piece of concrete, then let it fall. None of the other coffins were smashed.

"Somebody must have really hated this guy," Jacque said, as he kicked around some small chunks of rubble.

"Did she destroy what you needed?" Leif stepped up next to her.

"No, but she tried." Ari moved to an empty spot in the back corner. "I moved him after Remy bitched and moaned. But also, I didn't like anyone knowing where he was."

"Who?" Jacque asked, after he joined them.

"You'll see. Can I have my bag?"

Leif pulled the messenger bag from over his body and handed it to her. She pulled out a few things along with the large rough-cut amethyst. She had performed the reveal spell enough times that she could do it in her sleep. One hand hovered over the empty space, the other flicked a clear liquid from a vial. All while she said the spell. And like a polaroid picture after a few shakes, the form of a body appeared under a sheet.

Ari pulled the dust covered sheet with a flourish. Big mistake. It felt like she was about to cough up a lung. She wiped the grit out of her eyes, but still could barely see.

"That was cool. Dusty, but cool. Is he alive?" Jacque leaned in to inspect the man.

Ari grabbed Haviland under the arms and Leif grabbed his feet. "Let's move him over there." She nudged her chin out towards the partially clear area.

They laid the big man down gently. Ari pulled out a small leather-bound book, sage stick, and a candle. She handed Jacque the small orange medicine bottle.

"Pour a circle around us." Jacque popped the top and tiny white pellets of salt fell out.

Ari lit the sage stick and mumbled a cleansing spell. Goddess knew the entire cemetery needed it. But this would do for now.

"Leif, you'll have to say the spell with me. I'll look like I'm asleep for most of it." She pointed to the book propped open with a rock. "Say those words to bring us back." She laid down inside the salt circle with her hand over Haviland's chest with the amethyst between them and her head on his shoulder. To get comfortable she threw a leg over his.

"Know him that well, did you?" Leif lifted a brow.

Ari lifted her head and eyed him. "I might have. Now, fifteen minutes. I should be able to find him in that time. Hold the candle over us and say the spell. Do the same when it's time to return."

Leif and Ari began the chant to enter Otherworld and in less than a minute, she landed flat on her back with a splat. She pushed herself up on a muddy heap. At least, she hoped it was mud. It covered her arms up to the elbows. She flung it away from her and some still managed to hit her in the face.

"Great."

She looked down and she was wearing a beautiful white dress and purple satin flowers. She pulled the skirt around to inspect it, all brown. Thunder sounded in the distance, then the lightning lit up the dark sky. Just her luck, that man would be standing in the middle of a hurricane.

"Whatever, it's not even real." She flexed her arms, trying to loosen up. Then closed her eyes and thought of Haviland.

A deluge of warm water poured over Ari's head. She opened her eyes, and she stood at the base of a maelstrom. Torrential rain, dark clouds, thunder and lightning all swirled above her. Haviland floated above her with his arms spread wide in the eye of the storm.

"Haviland!" Ari cupped her hands to yell over the wind and rain.

He looked down upon her as if she was an ant.

"Come down here," Ari called out to him again. "Please."

The thunder and lightning stopped, but the clouds continue to churn around them. "Why?! You took her from me."

"I didn't. Come down here and talk to me." She was getting a crick in her neck from looking up at him.

He seemed to contemplate talking to her, then he floated down. "Why did you come here? To gloat? Tell me she's with someone else? That would make my prison complete."

His Irish brogue made it nearly impossible to understand him, but Ari caught the gist of it.

"That's not why I'm here."

"Why, then?"

She had to try a different tact. He was so angry and rightly so. He was in this prison because of his misguided love of her.

"Did you know Nyah had magic when you knew her?"

Haviland's head snapped around. "No, she didn't." His words were said with passion and confidence. "Her father told me."

"Well, men aren't the best judges all the time. Especially, when it comes to helpless females. He thought her incapable because she couldn't walk."

The assuredness on his face slipped a little. "What was her power then? I never saw her perform any type of magic and we were married."

I'm sure she used it every day, Ari thought. "Persuasion."

"That's not magic. Preachers and politicians, do it all the time." He laughed it off.

"Think about it. Did she touch you, then tell you to do something and you would," Ari said slowly.

"Of course, I did. I was her husband," Haviland snapped.

"Even if you had disagreed with her at first?"

He opened his mouth, then shut it. Seeming to really think about it. "Did she have you use your magic against people who had slighted her? Even for little things?"

"What does this have to do with her not wanting to be here? With me?"

"Nyah can walk and touch as many people as she likes now. I think she was making them go into a deep sleep. After she saw you and got the gift you gave her, everything started happening so fast. Nearly half the city…"

"I got the ruby from an old crone more than a hundred years ago. It was Nyah's favorite color, but she said it helped enhanced mental clarity." He gave a dry laugh. "She said, it would make my dreams come true."

"Goddess, Hav." Ari walked away with her hands on her hips. "You gave her the key to our destruction."

"How's that?"

"She's stolen Buster's necromancy. At least most of it. Enough to clear out every cemetery in town and destroy Houston."

"Why should I care? She's your problem now. I'm here and the place is growing on me." Haviland snapped his fingers.

The small hurricane above them disappeared and the sounds of crashing waves took its place. Green sand beach stretched out as far as the eye could see. Not a cloud in the big blue sky.

"She said, you were of no more use to her. That you did what she commanded." Ari knew that word would fire him up. "Now, she doesn't need you. She's powerful enough to destroy you." She threw that last in for good measure.

"She said, what?" Haviland shook his head. "Commanded me? Destroy me?"

He mumbled all this to himself a few times as if he couldn't believe it. Ari knew her time had to be almost up. She had to try.

"Come back with me. Help us." When he didn't respond she

pressed on. "Brennan talks about you. How you used to be before your marriage. You sounded like a good person. Find out what she did to you. She left you here to rot. I'm giving you a chance to make it right."

"Won't your white witches turn on you if you release me?"

"Let me worry about that," Ari said, then looked up.

The sun had gotten brighter and she could hear Leif whisper the start of the spell. "Take my hand if you want out. Take my hand and I will help you get revenge."

He stared at her outstretched palm but didn't move.

She looked up, then back at him. "Please, Haviland. I need you."

The beach, the water, the salty air disappeared. From one moment to the next the spell took her in a wash of bright whiteness.

CHAPTER 32

"Ari? Are you okay?" A cool hand touched her cheek. "She's not moving."

"Did you do the spell correctly?" Jacque said holding her hand.

Ari groaned. "Yeah, he did it, right." Two pairs of hands helped her sit up.

"I'm happy you're okay." Leif gave her a quick kiss. Then looked at the still unmoving body next to her. "Did he agree?"

Ari looked at the older Haviland and all the feelings of the younger version she knew came flooding back. She touched the gray hair, then his cheek.

"I'd hoped he would. Nyah treated him so wrong and he didn't even know it. She thought his magic was strong enough to cure her, that's why she married him and as she was dying she sent him on an impossible mission."

"To bring her back." Haviland grabbed her hand and placed it over her heart. When their eyes met, he continued, "So, all of these years? Centuries? I was under her control."

Ari knew it wasn't a question, but she nodded all the same. "I'm sorry."

He pushed himself up. "What is, is. Let's find her and I'll do the rest." He stood up and extended a hand.

Jacque and Leif extended their hands as well. Ari looked at all of them, then reached for Leif and Jacque. "Thank you."

"You've seemed to have acquired a few more men since we were together." Haviland smirked.

"Stop that. We were never together."

Haviland stared at Jacque. "Is he safe to be around?"

"Technically, he's safer than you." Ari slid the amethyst into her pocket and threw everything else into her bag. "Come on fellas, we have a city to save."

Ari intertwined her fingers with Leif as they headed for the exit. For an instant, Ari's heart swelled with hope, but it was dashed by six simple words.

"Daughter, so good to see you."

"Erissa." An explosion boomed. Ari flinched. Now, that sounded like a bomb had just gone off. "I don't have time for this. The city is burning."

So much had happened tonight but seeing her mother in a decimated cemetery topped the list. Erissa stood with a few members of the security team of the Black-Blood coven and Ella Grace. Leif's fingers slid from hers, but the absence was felt through her entire body. She couldn't delve into that at the moment.

"I don't care about the dismages. This witch is doing me a favor. And with his power." She tipped her head towards Haviland. "I can rule them as well."

"I told you he would lead you to the ancient witch. You did good, Leaves." Ella Grace said, with a huge smile.

Ari stared at him. "I was a mission?"

"Of course, you were. Leif is a loyal member of the Black Blood coven. He does what he's told."

"Leif, is this the truth? You loyal to a group who would torture their own? Is that the kind of life you want?"

Leif looked between the two women but didn't move.

"Come back to your family, Leif," Erissa said.

Finally, he moved to stand next to Ari. Ella Grace screamed like someone had physically assaulted her. "Leif, No! She doesn't love you like I do."

"You sure you want me as an enemy, boy?" Erissa growled.

"She's my home. Ari is my family, now." He slid his hand into hers.

"Move. Let me through." Bodies shuffled as a woman fought her way through the crowd. "Where is my son?"

Ari recognized the well dressed, petite woman from the New Orleans coven and her overdressed witches. They should have been ready to pass out wearing those three-piece suits. They looked fantastic, but goodness, didn't they realize they were in Texas, now? October was not a cool month like in a lot of other states. They still had summer temps going on.

Jacque moved from the rear of their group and stood next to her. "Mom?"

"When Tatum said you had a psyphon with you, I knew there couldn't be that many in town. I called Alexandra to let her know you found her son. Your fiancé. Thank you, daughter."

Ari slowly turned. "Jacque? What the hell?" she whispered to him.

He hunched his shoulders. "I didn't know it was you," Jacque whispered.

"Your what?" Leif stared at Ari.

Ari rolled her eyes. "Look, I already told you I'm not marrying anyone. And this is certainly not the time." She moved to leave.

Erissa pulled a long hair-stick out and extended it towards Ari. The tip glowed in a cold, white magic. Ari's body surged with power in response and blue flames consumed her hands.

"Calm down, Ari," Jacque whispered.

"That's new," Haviland said looking at her hands.

Another explosion shook the foundation. "We don't have time for this," Ari said.

"No, we don't." Erissa twirled the tip of her wand.

Multiple projectiles flew through the air. Ari's shield bracelet lit up as each dart came in contact with it. Haviland's hand slid around her waist from behind her. She couldn't tell if he was trying to find protection under her shield, but she wouldn't put it past him to cop a feel.

Warmth touched her ear when her old boyfriend spoke. "You have an exit strategy?"

As much as she missed Heath, having Haviland's hand on her was not the same. She pried his hand from her body. The smell of the smoke tingled her nose. Gray plumes filled the sky from every direction now. The constant wails of sirens could be heard in the distance, along with steady barrage of popping noises. Ari was positive those were gunshots and not fireworks.

If the police were shooting at the walking dead, then they were trying to fight magic with bullets. That was a war they couldn't win.

Instead of engaging the coven, she needed to save her strength for the real battle. Ari kept looking ahead as she spoke to Jacque.

"Jacque?"

"Yes?" He responded without looking at her.

"You okay to use your powers? We gotta go. I mean your coven…"

Jacque extended his left hand. "They'll be fine." When he thrust out his right hand, he said, "You might want to take a step back."

The NOLA coven must have known what his hand being out meant. They didn't have to hear him to know they needed to move.

"And don't…" Ari said as she complied, pushing Haviland back as well.

"Kill them. I know," Jacque finished.

A few of the Black Blood coven watched the NOLA coven. Erissa looked up at Jacque, then at the gap between the covens. Before she could open her mouth, to maybe order a retreat, her wand fell out of her hand and the entire Black Blood coven crumbled to their knees.

"In my hundreds of years, I'd only heard of a psyphon. Never seen one in action. Very interesting, your friend," Haviland said with awe in his voice.

Jacque walked down the steps, with his hands still focused on the downed coven. Ari, Leif, and Haviland followed him, then ran for the car.

Ari started Tiffany up, then leaned over and opened the passenger side door. "Jacque, get in the car."

Jacque snapped his hands closed, then all but fell into the car. The tires kicked up dirt and rocks as they sped out of the cemetery, leaving the Black Blood coven laid out unconscious on the ground.

"You okay?" Ari said.

Jacque nodded. "Ari, I can feel some intense magical energy that way." He pointed towards the area with the most fires. That entire side of town was lit by plumes of smoke, along with an intense orange and yellow light.

The streets were littered with debris, bones, and bodies. She couldn't tell if they were coma victims or newly risen from the dead. Buildings were on fire, or smoke smoldered in others.

Jacque grunted and nodded as she maneuvered the streets to find Nyah. When they reached the sea of fires that lit up the massive park near the I-10 freeway and burning, walking skeletons, they knew they had to be close.

All the burning buildings looked the same at this point. Ari just tried to not run anyone over, living or dead.

"Pull over," Jacque said. "She's there."

The stand-alone skyscraper wasn't on fire. The picturesque Greek inspired water-wall next to it even continued to flow with a glowing pristine white light, unmolested by the filthy creatures from the cemetery.

Ari stopped the car in the middle of the street in front of the tall blue obelisk-style building with bright light circling the city. The first line of defense were people with dead eyes in hospital gowns. They spanned the entire block in a straight line. The living dead surrounded the building, blocking their way inside from every direction.

Dust kicked up around them. A small tornado engulfed Haviland. Ari's first thought was that he was running away. But when the dust settled, she saw a face she'd been trying to forget for the past six months.

Heath.

Haviland transformed into the man she'd met and dated. He flexed his fingers, then bent over and stretched. Basically, he looked like he was having a Richard Simmons moment when he began to run in place.

"Oh, that's much better. This body works so much better. Now, if I had my staff, I'd get us in." Haviland said.

"We don't want to kill them," Ari said hotly.

"Look around, Love. They are already dead." Haviland waved his hand to all of the still bodies in from of the building.

"Not all of them. Some of them are innocent in all of this. If you had your staff would you just kill everybody?"

Haviland gave a long exaggerated sigh. "If it would make you happy, then, no, I wouldn't kill everybody."

Ari looked at the deep blue eyes that nearly looked black and the shoulder length jet black hair with the two long white streaks at his temples. He looked like her Heath, but he wasn't. She used to believe everything he said, but she knew better.

She looked around at what they were facing and knew they needed every advantage. She walked to the back of Tiffany and popped the trunk. There wasn't much there: a case of water she was too lazy to take out from the last time she went to the grocery store, reusable cloth shopping bags, and a blanket. She threw the colorful material back to reveal a six-foot wooden staff.

Ari walked towards the men with the large stick in her hands. Haviland's eyes stared at it.

"Here." Ari held the staff out to him. "I think we're going to need all the help we can get."

Haviland took it carefully from her grasp, holding it with reverence. "Hello, my old friend. I knew she would take care of you."

"Um, yeah. It's been in my trunk this entire time."

"No matter. I have it now. Are we ready?" Haviland caressed the runes carved into the top of the staff.

"One second," Jacque said right before he grabbed Ari's hand

and pulled her out of earshot of the other two men. "I'm feeling too much power. I think you guys need more power. I have an idea, but do you trust them?"

Ari looked up towards Leif and Haviland, who had the face of Heath right now. Her ex and current boyfriend. Both with sketchy pasts, but she cared for them both dearly.

"Yes. Now, what are you thinking?"

"This Nyah is more powerful than any witch I've come across. I still have your coven's power coursing through me."

She began to shake her head before he finished telling her his plan, because she had a good idea what he wanted to do. "That's so much power."

"You guys will need it. Without it, I don't think any of us will make it out of this alive."

Ari nodded and they walked back to the others.

"Jacque has a plan." She nodded in his direction.

"Everyone, hold hands," Jacque said, with his hands out.

Ari grabbed his immediately. But Leif and Haviland looked at Jacque, then their hands.

"No offense Ari, but you do realize what happens when you touch a psyphon?" Leif said.

"I am well aware. Now, the question is, do you trust me?"

"You know I do," Leif said.

She held her free hand out to him and after a long minute he took it. Haviland eyed them all. "Fine." He grabbed both Jacque and Leif's hands.

Jacque closed his eyes and tightened his hand on Ari's when the power began to flow. Her hand warmed, then a jolt of energy flowed through them all. Each person in the small circle flinched and pulled at their interconnected hands.

The new magic flowing through Ari didn't hurt or burn, but it felt like she had eaten so much that she could burst at any moment.

"No… more." Ari strained out.

The entire group let out a collective scream as they broke apart and fell to the ground.

After a minute or two to catch their breath, Haviland spoke first.

He looked at his hands. Little lightning bolts crackled over his hands. “What. The hell. Was that?”

“Psyphons don’t only take power, we can give it as well,” Jacque said, still breathing hard.

“You should be the most powerful witch among us all.”

Jacque shook his head. “I can’t keep it or use it. It just fades away.”

Haviland nodded sagely. “What’s next?”

“I’ll cause a diversion. You guys should be able to handle a few of them and get in.”

At the top of skyscraper, a huge, bright light extended to the city edges, like a lighthouse's beacon, but out towards a sea of cement, buildings, and people. The beacon circled the city, illuminating all it touched with a brilliant white radiance. Upon the light's next revolution, everything turned a deep shade of red. Everyone looked up, including the living dead and possessed.

“Is that the ruby? Why is she using it there? I don't understand.” Ari asked, still looking up.

“The old witch said it helped with mental clarity or maybe that it cleared mental pathways all together. I'm not sure now,” Haviland said as he got off the ground.

"What? That's crazy," Leif chimed in.

“Hind-sight, my boy. Wasn't like I knew she was planning on taking over the world with it," Haviland said.

"So, the light. It could make us forget everyone? Everything?" Ari asked.

"I think maybe more like them." Haviland pointed to the johnny-wearing possessed people. "I'm not sure. You can ask her when we get up there. It’s now or never. And I personally feel the need for a bit of revenge.”

Haviland extended his staff like Moses and parted the people like the Red Sea. It was like an invisible wall held them back. Haviland's staff was great but it couldn't hold off the hundreds of dead blocking the entry. Jacque drew the attention of the line of skeleton warriors.

It was time to rumble.

CHAPTER 33

The stylings of Michael Bublé blared through the lobby speakers. Ari walked in a wide circle as she looked upward. The atrium seemed to go on for miles. As peaceful as everything seemed at the moment, potted plants were knocked over, small trees had been trampled, seating areas were pushed aside as if an ocean of people had gone through.

Leif pulled her by the hand. "Come. It's a long way up."

Haviland stood holding his old staff at the stairwell door. "She'll kill everyone if we don't get to her."

These men had lost their minds if they thought she was about to traipse up sixty-four flights of stairs. She would die before the fifth floor.

"Haven't you guys noticed." Ari waved at the air above her head. They both had blank faces. "You take the stairs if you want. I'm going to do this." Ari pressed the button to the elevator and a bell sounded as the doors slid open.

"Why they hell didn't you say something earlier," Haviland said, as he got into the elevator.

"Impressive." Leif raised a brow.

A fine misting of soil covered the floor. Ari scratched her shoe, smiled, then pressed the button to the largest number without answering him. Her fire, and the guys' cold and electrical powers, crackled within the small space.

The first elevator had taken them halfway up, and this elevator took them the rest of the way. The doors slid open, but no one moved at first. Ari looked at both of the guys, and when they still imitated statues, she took a step. Leif flung his hand out covering Ari's stomach, stopping her forward motion. Haviland held out his staff, the tip glowed a soft orange as he held the elevator open. He stepped out alone looking both ways with the staff extended. When no skeleton warriors rushed him, Ari and Leif followed.

The small group fanned out through the large office area.

Haviland tossed a phone across the hallway as he stormed out. "It's just a regular office floor. Where?"

"Hey guys." Ari stepped out from a small alcove. "I think this is it."

Ari pulled on the heavy metal door hanging off the hinges. In block red lettering, the door read, 'No entry - Observation'. They were two floors below the beacon light level. Next to the broken door, a small placard showed a stick man walking up stairs.

Haviland gave her a nod and ran up the stairs two at a time.

Leif grabbed Ari's hand and pulled her back. "You okay?"

"Yeah." Ari nodded. "You ready?"

He squeezed her hand and nodded. It was time to enter the fray. They turned to head up the stairs when the elevator dinged.

"It must be Jacque. Go ahead, we'll catch up," Ari said, then walked back down the stairs.

"You sure. I can wait," Leif said, from the first landing.

Ari waved him off. "I'm sure he needs help. Watch out for his staff."

Leif took off and Ari walked back to the bank of elevators. The doors had closed, but no one was there.

"Jacque? Where are you?" Ari walked back and forth looking around.

"I knew you would be here."

Ari froze. *Why was he here?* She turned around slowly to see the absolute last person she thought she'd see.

Detective Adam Westin.

GLASS SHATTERED, the building shook, and the lights flickered. Ari and Detective Westin braced themselves against the wall. Particles from the ceiling floated down like snowflakes.

"You have to get out of here." Ari tapped the down button. "It's not safe."

"And it's safe for you? I'm hearing voices. They're fucking zombies terrorizing the city and you know why. What's going on up there?" He moved towards the broken door and Ari blocked his path.

"You can't." A loud boom echoed through the stairwell. She looked up, then back at him.

"You go. I go." Westin folded his arms, shaking his head.

"You're going to get yourself killed."

He was just a man. She needed to protect him, whether she liked him or not. Without thought, she reached for him. The words to bespell him hung on her lips.

He moved out of her reach. "I know you did something to me before. I got protection this time." He pulled a hamsa hand with a tiger eye necklace from under his shirt. "I don't completely believe in this woogie witchy stuff. But the voices…" He trailed off with a head shake.

"She's no longer telling you what to do," Ari said sadly. She could only wonder what Nyah made him do.

"How did you know?" He shook his head like he wanted to say more but couldn't. "Never mind. Are we going or what?"

That was the question. From what she could hear, the battle wasn't over. And she had to do what she could. There was no way she was letting Nyah take over.

"Fine," Ari said as she threw her hands up.

She saw the resolve in his eyes and there was nothing she could do to stop him. She wanted to tell him a list of things about magic, wrap him in bubble wrap, and beat into his head that his necklace couldn't protect him from everything. But in the end, she just said, "Watch yourself."

They ran up the two flights of stairs into the battle.

CHAPTER 34

Piles of frozen broken bones blocked the entrance to the Observation deck. Ari stepped over the pile, only to step on a ribcage. It crumbled under the weight of her foot. The beacon blazed a bright white.

Well, at least that went right, Ari thought.

A line of lightning flew past her head. She ducked just in time. She turned to see the scorch mark in the wall near Detective Westin. She gave him the 'I told you so' look.

She looked around just in time to catch sight of Leif. Power flooded her body and her fists lit up like little tiki torches. She blasted two fire balls off and knocked two possessed coma patients off of him. They were after something he held. The glint of red caught her eye within the ball of ice. Leif smiled and tossed the ball before succumbing to the rush of possessed people coming at him.

"No!" Nyah screamed.

Ari caught the soccer ball sized ball of ice. She couldn't hold on to it and nearly dropped it. She cradled it into in her shirt and wiped away some of the condensation. The headdress with the ruby glistened back at her. When she looked up, her eyes met her old roommate's.

"I believe you have something of mine." Nyah held her hand out. "I won't kill them if you give me what I want."

Ari looked around the room, so many lives were already lost. Haviland was locked in battle with three skeletons. One creature's mouth opened unusually wide and bit down on his shoulder. Ari's hand lit a bright orange, but Nyah stood in her path.

"Nyah, please, just stop this now," Ari pleaded. She'd said the words, but honestly, she didn't know what she was asking for. Nyah wouldn't give up this power now that she'd had it. Deep in her heart, she knew there was only one way this could end.

The corner of Nyah's mouth quirked up. "You are amusing." Her eyes flicked to something behind Ari. "You. Grab her."

Ari turned to see Detective Westin holding his head. He was struggling. "Fight it. Fight her," Ari whispered. She turned back to Nyah, then lifted the ice ball. "If you want this, then release him."

Nyah waved a hand and Westin fell to the floor on all fours. "Now, give it."

A shot rang out and Nyah screamed. Detective Westin's gun was still poised on Nyah who touched the blood streaming down her arm. She focused on the downed detective. "I show you mercy and this is how you repay me?"

The gun in the detective's hand began to vibrate. Westin's eyes enlarged when the barrel turned towards his face. Ari's hand shot out just as Nyah said, "Shoot."

A bloom of red covered the detective's left shoulder. He laid unconscious against the wall. Ari couldn't tell if he was alive or not, but she had to focus on the woman before her.

Power flooded Ari's hand and the ice turned to water as it melted away. She held the date sized ruby between two fingers and the last pieces of metal from the headdress liquified.

Nyah's eyes went wide, avarice clear in her eyes. "Why do you hide such power?"

"Power isn't the key to happiness." Ari shook her head like she was disappointed in a child. "I tried to show you that."

"Helping old people? Reading tarot to losers? No, my dear, Aria, this is power." She held her hands aloft and the undead and others stopped moving. "Life and death. Right here…" she held her hand out palm up, and curled a finger.

One possessed hospital patient walked towards her. His eyes had the blank stare they all had. Nyah patted his cheek and whispered something in his ear. The bald man blinked, then looked around. Ari knew the instant he woke up. His eyes widened at the carnage at his feet, then to the scene around him.

"What is this?" the bald man asked over and over. "This can't be real."

"Nyah, don't do this." Ari shook her head.

Nyah snapped her fingers as if she were bored and the bald man suddenly dropped. "He was dying anyway. I could smell it on him. I put him out of his misery." She whipped her hand out and the fighting reconvened.

"It was you. The illness. The city falling into a coma?" Pain lanced through Ari at the thought of so many people dead and hurt and for what? "Why?"

"No, not me. Well, not at first. Did you know Buster never used even a fraction of his power. His necromancer blood brought me back and tied us together. But once I got the ruby, everything clicked into place. I could change the world, but I needed an army and I got it. Look around, Aria. This city… is mine."

"My name is Ari. You should at least be able to say my name right after all this time!"

Nyah gave a smile that showed far too many teeth. "Ari," she threw her hands wide and closed her eyes for a moment, "let me show you real power."

Ari felt a pulse of ice-cold power extend through the room.

"What did you just do?" Ari looked around.

Nyah gave another toothy smile, before saying, "I'm ending this."

Leif crawled out from under a pile of stiff bodies. A light sheen sparkled on them. He froze them. He lifted a hand once he was completely clear of the heap. Ari lifted her head in Haviland's direction and Leif winked in response.

It was now, before the next batch of undead made it to them. All the extra magic Jacque had given them was nearly gone. She used all her strength to throw the ruby across the room.

"This game is over. You've lost." Nyah turned to follow the gem's path.

Haviland snatched it out of the air, and held the small red gem up to the light. "All of this trouble because of this."

"Not just that." Nyah moved like a snake towards Haviland. "Now, I have power. I can do anything." Her voice had become a sultry purr. "We can do anything. Conquer anyone. Just like that." She snapped her fingers.

Haviland seemed to considerate it. "Sorry, Ari." He clicked the ruby into his staff.

"Haviland, no! You promised." Ari felt a flood of tears build in her.

Nyah touched Haviland's chest and turned back to give Ari an evil smile. "I told you. You lost." She turned her face up to kiss Haviland.

The couple floated up. Haviland's arm tightened around Nyah. His fingers released the staff as he deepened the kiss with Nyah. The staff didn't fall, Ari was ready with her hands extended to control the staff's descent. It weebled and wobbled, but it didn't hit the ground. She let out a soft exhale. When this was over, she was really going to work on her telekinesis.

Ari and Leif put their hands on the staff and began the spell Haviland had drilled into them on the sixty-two-floor elevator ride. The power swirled around the room and Nyah broke the kiss, but not from Haviland's grip.

"What are you doing?" Nyah struggled.

"Ending this." Haviland stabbed Ari's athame under her ribcage. "I love you. Always." He caressed her cheek.

Nyah lifted her hand and knocked his fingers away, as a tear ran down. "Never. Loved."

Magic surged out from her body in two visible arcs. One a crystalline blue, the other golden. He floated back down and laid her body gently on top of the debris.

Ari watched him with sad eyes, but kept her hands on the staff. "I'm so sorry."

Haviland gave a tight nod, then placed his hands on the staff as well. "Shall we finish this?"

They all held a portion of the staff with two hands. Ari looked at Leif and Haviland, and with a wordless smile, she thanked them. They each poured power into the staff, and a bright red color filled the observation deck like a mini sun, sans the heat.

The ruby pulsed and the runes along the side of the staff went from a faint pink to a deep red. Ari took control of the staff with her mind and moved it out of the window. And just in time, the ruby exploded, taking the staff with it. A fine misting of red crystals and wood-splinters were carried away on the wind. Ari doubted if any of it made it to the ground.

Haviland looked at Nyah's body. "I'll take her back. You should check on your friend."

Oh, goddess, Buster. She hadn't had time to think about his fate. Now she understood everything he was struggling with. "Thank you. Sorry."

Ari wanted to say more, but Haviland pulled her into a fierce hug. Her arms hung limp for a moment, then circled his waist.

"No, go raibh maith agat. I think I'm going to go home and rest," Haviland whispered in her ear. He pulled out of her grasp and really looked at Ari. "You… keep my books. I won't need them anymore."

With that he picked up Nyah's body and stepped out through the broken window to the observation deck, then stepped off.

Ari and Leif turned to the gasp behind them.

"Did he just? How could you let him?" Detective Westin hobbled to his feet to look out. Holding his arms close to his body.

"What? No? He's fine." Ari waved at the open space where Haviland stepped off.

Ari watched Westin move slowly around the clutter. Good to know he was just knocked out and not dead. "Are you alright?" She pointed towards the bloody shirt.

He looked down, then touched the area. "It looks worse than it is. A scratch."

Ari rolled her eyes. Men always said that.

"Too bad we can't exit the building like that," Leif said with a smile as he looked at the bodies blocking the door.

"So true."

Ari looked around the room with her hands on her hips. A pile of bones near the entrance moved and then another in the back corner moved. Flames coated her hands, a cool breeze circled the room, and out the corner of her eye, she could see that the detective had pulled his service weapon. The heap of bones at the door fell inward, and Jacque tumbled in.

"Stars above, Jacque. We could have killed you." Ari shook her hands and the flames died away.

Jacque raised his hands. "Only person who could kill me is probably him." He pointed with one finger past Ari.

Everyone turned to Detective Westin.

"Detective?" Ari lifted a brow when he didn't move.

He lowered it but didn't put it away.

"The zombies just dropped dead a few minutes ago. They were hellbent on getting up here, then nothing."

A hand popped out of the stack of bones and debris. Leif grabbed it and pulled the person out. A dark-haired young woman in a hospital-johnny, covered in soot and filth emerged. Tears streamed down the young lady's face, then a squeaky, familiar voice began to ramble about 'not knowing how she got there' and 'where was she now.'

"Brittania, is that you?" Ari wiped at her face. "Take a deep breath."

The young woman's big blue eyes were the only thing that was recognizable.

"Ari?" She paused for all of two-seconds, then the water works started all over again as she cried on Ari's shoulder.

The men, all of the sudden were busy with looking for other survivors far away from them. Leaving her with the hysterical woman. Ari's shoulder was soaked, and her ears were close to bleeding. Fed up, she murmured a spell in Brittania's ear and the girl fell asleep holding on to Ari. She eased her down near the door.

"What did you do to her?" Westin checked her pulse.

"Nothing. I think all of this was just too much. Now, we need to check for survivors before we go."

"Is that what you did to me?" He stared at her intently, but a hint of fear clouded his eyes.

"Detective, look. I've done nothing but try to protect you."

"I don't need protection." Westin cut in angrily. "I need the truth!"

"Fine. Look around you. This is the truth. You saw it with your own eyes and heard it with your own ears. If you still don't believe in 'mumbo jumbo witchy stuff'." She used air quotes for the last. "Then I don't know what to tell you."

She looked around at the busted beacon light, broken glass, and skeletons. They couldn't fix this with magic. All they could do now was find survivors and check on family and friends.

"Check the rubble. Any more survivors, we're taking them to the hospital. The sun will be up soon."

CHAPTER 35

Who knew people, dead or alive, could do so much damage? The small group of survivors walked out into the abandoned streets. Ari looked at the growing number of people and Tiffany. Not everyone could fit in her car. A wide-eyed, dark-haired young man had his arm over Brittania's shoulder. He limped along to the curb, then with a hand around his waist, Britt helped ease him to the ground.

Britannia walked over to Ari. She looked back at the man, then turned her back to the guy and whispered. "I think his arm is broken, Ari. Is there any way to get him to the hospital?"

"We are trying to find some transportation." Ari looked intently in both directions.

The Dukes of Hazzard car horn blared through the silence. A purple and blue low rider truck pulled up in front of the girls. Leif followed in an old, rusty Silverado, without no sound effects.

"You need a ride?" With the window rolled down, Detective Westin banged the door with his one good hand.

"How did you get this?" Ari looked in the back of the truck. Empty. Great.

"I borrowed it," the detective said as he got out.

"Borrowed? Can a man in your position do that?" Ari lifted a brow.

"Commandeered. Whatever. These are extenuating circumstances. We'll put it back once we get these people to the hospital."

With that, Ari, Leif and Jacque loaded the survivors in the bed of the trucks and a couple in her car. Britannia rode in the truck with her charge. Ari smiled and knew Britannia's visits would be few and far between now, judging by the smile on her face and the gleam in her eyes for the man next to her.

Bodies and bones littered the streets. They drove around overturned cars and trucks and emergency vehicles. Not everyone had been turned into destructive, mindless zombies. Firemen and women were putting out building fires and the police pulled bodies from the stacks of debris.

It took twice as long to get to the medical center, but when they arrived it didn't look nearly as bad as the Galleria area they had just left. Her friends kept the hospitals from being set on fire or destroyed.

They dropped the survivors off at the parking lot triage. Detective Westin followed them away from the crowd.

"Detective, you need to have that shoulder looked at." Ari nodded towards his arm.

"In a minute. I just want to say—"

"You're sorry," Ari supplied.

"No." He shook his head. "That I see now that there are more things in this world that I don't understand. But I need to be prepared. So, after this heals, you will tell me everything." He turned and walked away.

"Detective Westin. Westin!"

When he finally looked back, he said, "Can you return the truck? Thanks."

The man was so stubborn but she couldn't stop him. Who knew, maybe he would get off her back, now.

"Guys, I want to find Buster."

"You want us to go with?" Jacque looked between him and Leif.

"No, I'm fine. I'm going home right after. I'm exhausted." Ari squeezed his hand. His eyes still lit up whenever she touched him, and it warmed her heart.

"I'll go return the truck then." Jacque waved as he walked away.

Leif wrapped her in his arms. "You okay?"

"Yeah, just tired. But I want to see Buster, let him know that we're good," Ari said.

"I'll see you back at your place in a little while." Leif said, and she nodded.

He leaned in and pressed his lips to hers, nothing scandalous, more like I'm-happy-we're-alive kind of kiss.

Ari went on her search for Buster. He was no longer in a room. She had to use magic to find him. The simple locator spell was something she used as a child to find her toys. She whispered the words, then something like an invisible string tugged her around the hospital to a nurse's station on the sixth floor. People in scrubs moved about in a hurry and the severely injured filled the hallway on gurneys. But no Buster.

"Excuse me," Ari said to the first nurse who paused. "Is there a Buster Calaveras on this floor?"

"There's no way…" the nurse started to move away from the desk.

"Please, could you look?" Ari blocked her path.

The nurse exhaled loudly, then said, "Fine. Calaveras, you said?" Her fingers flew across the keypad. "He should still be here. Check down in room D." She pointed down the hall. "It's through the double doors. Sorry, I couldn't be more help."

Ari nodded and thanked her before the woman walked away. She stepped into a room wall to wall with bandaged people, but no Buster. She turned with her hands on her hips.

"Excuse me." A kid of five, maybe six stood next to her.

"Yes, sir." Ari squatted down to look him in the eye.

"Are you Ms. Ari?"

"Yes." She nodded. "How did you know that?"

"He said you'd come," the kid said.

"Who said?"

"The nice man with long hair. Here, this is for you." He held out a folded piece of yellow lined paper.

She took the paper, and the kid went back to his chair next to a sleeping woman.

She walked back to Tiffany before she opened the letter. Her eyes whisked over the brief message.

"How can I ask for forgiveness, when I can't forgive myself? Until I can do that, I can't face you. You were right to curse me. I deserved that and more. Bust-A-Sud is yours, the lawyer will call you soon. This won't be a fast process, but I'll get there. Take care."

Ari wiped away the tears. Didn't that goof know that she would've forgiven him? That she had forgiven him. It wasn't his fault. But she understood. She had to be patient for her friend to return.

All the stress washed through her in a flood of tears and exhaustion. After a good cry she headed home. She felt like she could sleep for a week.

THE SMELL of bacon made Ari open her eyes and her stomach growl. She inhaled again. Was that coffee? Her heart stopped for a full five seconds or at least it felt that way. Had Nyah returned? And learned how to make coffee?

Not a chance.

A cool arm slid over her body sending a familiar chill up her spine.

"What's wrong?" She turned over to look at her ghostly best friend.

"It's been so long since it was just me and you?" His pale blue eyes stared into hers.

"I know."

"Those were the good ol' days."

Remy held his hand to her cheek even though he couldn't touch her, she felt him. He held a sadness that was nearly tangible, and it crushed her heart. She could tell this wasn't going to end well, no matter what he told her.

"Je suis désolé about telling her your secrets," he said.

"There's nothing to apologize for. You were under her spell. Now, tell me why you are really in this bed?"

"The house is full."

A pan crashed from another room in the house, presumably the kitchen. Then a lot of voices grumbled.

Remy lifted his brows. "Yeah. And Otherworld is empty. I just need some time alone et mais, I like the new guys. I know they'll keep you safe."

"Leif and—"

"Jacque."

The door opened. "Princess, you up?" Leif wiped his hands on a kitchen towel. He leaned against the door in a white t-shirt and jeans with a "Kiss the Witch" apron on.

She wiped a tear away, in what she thought was a smooth move into the sheet when she turned to look at him. "Just talking to Remy."

He looked around the room with a smile. "Morning Rem."

Remy smiled. "Oui, I like him, beaucoup."

"He said, 'Good morning.' What smells so good out there?"

"Peppered bacon, eggs, grits. A good southern breakfast. I've just put the biscuits in. You need to hurry. Your cousins will eat it all if you don't get out here."

Ari nodded with a smile. "That's so true. I'll be right out." She threw back the covers and eyed Remy. "You heard him. Food."

Remy lowered his head in a half bow, then disappeared. Ari quickly took a shower and dressed before her cousins ate everything.

THE FIRST THING that caught her eye was the cleared farm table. She almost didn't recognize it without the dirt spilled everywhere and pots. Then she heard a familiar voice.

"You want me to put on the kettle?" Elizabeth leaned out of the kitchen wiping her hands on a towel.

"Lizzy, I was worried when I didn't see you last night." Ari pulled her into an embrace. When they pulled apart, she squeezed her friend's arm and whispered, "Everything's okay?"

Elizabeth nodded. "I'm fine. Now, sit. Lucas might hurt us if we don't eat soon."

Ari ambled around the table, touching the napkins and silverware. "You guys. This is awesome."

"Where did all the dishes come from?" Ari wiped a tear away.

"Jacque brought some from his place and Elizabeth brought some over after I had tea with her yesterday," Leif said, as he pulled out the chair from the head of the table.

"Yesterday?"

Lucas grabbed a sausage link. "Yeah, Cuz, you've been out for like two days."

"Two?" Ari looked around, they all nodded. "Wow, what have I missed?"

When no one said anything, she looked at everyone. Each face looked like they'd been sucking on a lemon. The kettle whistled and Elizabeth went back to the kitchen.

Leif slid his hand into hers and patted it. "You might want to sit down."

Now, this was making her extremely nervous. She slid into the chair. "Just spit it out."

Still, Leif said nothing. Ari reached up and pulled him into the seat next to her. "What the hell happened?" *I was only asleep for two freaking days.* She wanted to scream but held her tongue.

"The New Orleans coven recognized you as the supreme power and high priestess in Houston," Leif said.

"I told mother, we weren't getting married," Jacque stepped forward. "And that I would follow only you."

"Oh, Jacque." *What have you done?*

"You accepted me." He looked at his hands, then around the room. "Your friends accepted me. You don't know how much this means. I've hidden what I was for so long. So," he wiped away a tear. "Thank you. And mother said if you ever need anything, they would have your back."

"Guess after that bit of news got out. Erissa burned down any place you frequented. With everything that happened the other night, no one could tell that it was set after. But your mother left a magical residue, so that you would know it was the coven."

"The White Cauldron?"

"The building protected itself," Elizabeth said with a smile. "No one has seen you with the other witches. But we strengthened their wards, just in case."

"My place was melted. I think Ella Grace had her hand in that," Leif said, then looked away.

She could tell he was hurting. He genuinely liked the girl. But Ella Grace wanted something he couldn't give her. *His heart.*

"You can stay here," Ari offered.

Leif shook his head. "I'm going to stay with Jacque for a little while."

Well, hell and damnation. She did not see that coming. But she was pretty sure this was his way of keeping him away from her. "Okay."

"You have a full house as is," Leif finished.

Ari nodded, then said, "You don't think I can avoid this thing with Erissa?"

"You know how Auntie is," Rum answered. "Look at what she did to us for a helping you. Now, you're threatening her power base, challenging her authority. Not a chance."

The hairs on Ari's neck stood up, then her stomach growled, cutting through the quiet. "I guess that's our cue. There's nothing we can do about Erissa right now, so we should eat."

It only took Lucas to pour half the bacon onto his plate to get everyone riled up. Pulling them out of their morose mood. They all laughed as the platters of food went around the table. This is what a family… a coven was supposed to look like, not whatever her mother was creating.

She wiped away the tears and two cool hands touched her. Remy at her shoulder and Leif squeezed her hand.

Leif mouthed, "You okay?"

When she nodded, he squeezed her hand again, then they both dug in.

CHAPTER 36

The city wasn't any better two days later. People wandered the streets, resembling zombies in earnest, but for all the wrong reasons. They picked up clothes, trash, and she knew they were just trying to get their lives back.

Ari drove by the senior facility, a sign on the door announced the place would be closed until further notice. She would have to keep checking back to find out what happened to everyone. Even Nurse Frankie had disappeared from the property.

She needed to do something to help get the city back on its feet. When she looked deep inside herself, she felt like this was her fault. Ari needed to make this right. She went back to the place where it all began.

Woodland Glen cemetery.

Everyone - the boys, the White Cauldron witches, even her cousins had volunteered to help when she talked about cleaning up the cemetery. As helpful as Leif and Jacque wanted to be, they didn't own a shovel between them. For the first time in a while, all of them had to do things the old-fashioned way.

Without magic.

That being said, the boys embarked on a journey to the hardware store for tools. Hopefully, they'd make it out alive.

The line of vehicles inside the cemetery surprised Ari. It wasn't just the witches from the White Cauldron, but other families. Men and boys righted headstones, heavy machinery covered plots, and a host of people were cleaning the grave markers and laying flowers down. The entire scene touched her heart and one small boy of five or six handed her flower. "It's dia de los muertos, did you know that?" he'd told her.

She hadn't known, but she would never forget it. Much like Samhain, this Day of the Dead will be celebrated. Every year.

Surprisingly, no one was at the O'Malley mausoleum. Ari tentatively touched the doors. No wards and the doors were solid on their hinges. She pushed the doors open to find a pristine area.

The stained-glass. Repaired.

The benches. Fixed and in place.

Floor. Swept and dust-free.

A bottle of Bushmill 21-year-old whiskey sat atop Royal O'Malley's coffin. He hadn't forgotten. It was the first drink she'd poured him when they first met. When she touched the bottle, a small piece of paper appeared with her name on it. Haviland had probably forgotten more spells than she'd known in her lifetime.

She unfolded the letter and touched the wispy writing.

Ari,

I do not say this lightly but thank you. You have helped me close a chapter in my life I thought would end differently. I see now I must make amends for all I have done in the name of love. This place was a mess. I fixed it as best as I could. Hope it's to your liking.

I have grown to like your city and I gift you one last thing. A way to fix what Nyah did. I cannot repair the buildings or memories but this one thing I can. You will need your coven, and as many as you can gather.

Live well.

Enjoy the whiskey. Sláinte.

H.

Ari looked at the second piece of paper. At a quick glance, there were formations, drawings, and runes along with her favorite language, Latin. It was a long extensive spell. "I'm going to need more witches. Preferably someone who loves Latin."

Ari walked outside holding the note. Two spirits appeared before her. Krista and her grandfather. The smile on the little girl's face could light up a room.

"Ari, he's here."

"I see." In her heart, Ari knew she should be sad that this man had passed away, but they were happy and had each other. How could she be sad about that?

"I'm sorry," Pauppen Miller said as he moved closer to her.

"For what?" Ari frowned.

"For not believing you, when you told me about my granddaughter."

Ari shook her head. "There's nothing to apologize for. I'm glad you're together now."

"Thanks." Krista wrapped her transparent arms around Ari and a cold chill went up her spine.

Ari said, "No problem." Even though this event had nothing to do with her.

They both disappeared in a blink and when she looked around, she spotted one of the boys.

"Jacque, you guys made it."

"Barely," Jacque said with a smile. "It was a crazy… mad house."

"I believe it. Where's Leif?" Ari looked around.

"Um, I believe he had to go back to the truck." Jacque pointed behind him. "He was passing out rakes and trash bags last I saw."

"Cool. Something's come up." When he cringed, she touched his arm. "Not like that, but I might need your mom's coven sooner than I thought."

He nodded with a smile. "She'll like that."

Ari walked towards the entrance.

FOR AS MANY people who were cleaning and working, it wasn't very loud. Maybe that's how she picked up the voices just outside the gates. Or maybe it was her scent. It burned her nose every time. Wild, disheveled hair covered most of her face, but even from the side she knew the girl.

"I knew you'd be here," Ella Grace said to Leif. "Following her around like a puppy."

"Ella Grace, what are you doing here?" Leif took a step towards her.

"At least you remember my name."

"E.G., what's going on?" Leif softened his voice. Much like talking to a wild animal.

"Why?" Ella Grace whispered through tears.

"Why, what?" Leif frowned, looking perplexed.

"Why her?!" Ella Grace stamped her foot. "Didn't we show you how horrible she was?"

Ari knew this wasn't good. But interrupting might make it worse. She leaned against the wall and continued to watch.

"We?" Leif shook his head. "We, who?"

Ella Grace went on like he hadn't asked her a question. "I met the woman your girlfriend has kept hostage in her home. Did you know that?"

Oh, shit. This just went from bad to worse. Ari wanted to drag Leif out of there. He couldn't see how dangerous the young girl was in this state.

"She told me how Ari murdered all those old people and at the washateria." Ella Grace paced, hitting her head with something in her hand. "I thought the police would arrest her, but no. She just kept getting away with murder."

"E.G., she didn't do those things. You called the police on her?"

"Look at you, defending her. She's bewitched you. My father created many potions for the coven; I'm sure I can find something to fix you. Leave her, come back to me." She held her hands out to him.

Then Ari could see them, Ella Grace held two clear containers; both filled with a bright green liquid.

"Why would you do all this Ella?"

The pleading in his voice nearly broke Ari's heart.

"The high priestess would kill me if I hurt her precious daughter. But she hurt the coven, Lady Tatum, my high priestess, then…" She looked at Leif with such longing in her eyes. "She took you away from me."

"Ella—" Leif started.

"No! Come back with me, now. They'll forgive you. The coven will take you back. I know they will." Her body convulsed as sobs racked through her. "I, I love—"

Leif shook his head. "Ella Grace." Cutting her off. "This isn't the way."

"It's the only way." Ella Grace's voice went to a solemn, nearly quiet tone. "Don't you see that."

Ari could see the young girl's resolve.

"No."

Ella Grace lowered her head as she popped the corks on the bottles and opened her arms to hug him. Leif didn't understand what he was about to walk into.

"Hey! Keep your hands off my man," Ari called out.

The bottles flew through the air, liquid coming towards her in streams. Ari's hands were already ready for the attack and she thrust them out and a beachball sized blue flame sent the liquid, the containers, and Ella Grace soaring through the air.

The girl hit the side of a truck. Her body crumpled to the ground, then she emitted a gut-wrenching scream that sounded like a wounded animal in pain.

"Ari, what did you do?" Leif looked between them.

Smoke rose from Ella Grace's hands and face. When she moved her hands, it revealed the broken glass embedded in her skin. When Leif moved towards her, she went into a frenzy.

"Ella, let me help you," Leif pleaded.

"Get away from me!" Her words sounded slurred as she threw out her good hand and pushed against the vehicle to get to her feet. "You let her do this to me. See what kind of person she is? I won't forget. Ever." She fumbled around in her pockets with her good hand and slammed another bottle on the ground.

The thick, black smoke blocked her from their sight. Leif blasted a cool breeze to clear the area, freezing everything in his path.

No sign of Ella Grace.

"What the hell just happened?" Leif stared at Ari.

"I think, no, I'm sure she was going to kill you both."

Leif shook his head in disbelief. "No. No."

"Leif. She was in love with you."

He opened his mouth to speak, then closed it. There were no words.

"I'm sure she'll get some help. She was strong enough to leave," Ari said to comfort him.

Leif nodded, but his face gave away nothing. She held her arms wide, because she couldn't think of anything else to do. He stood there long enough that she thought he wouldn't hug her, then he fell into her arms. No tears, but she felt the deep sigh he released before they pulled apart.

"You okay?"

He gave a tight nod, and a grim smile. She figured that was the best she was going to get under the circumstances.

"I think I may have a way to put all the bodies back." She held out Haviland's note.

"That reminds me, I went back to your place and found this taped to the building." He held out an envelope with her full name on it.

It was a note type of day. First Buster, then Haviland, now this. The only person she hadn't gotten a missive from was Leise. She opened it but didn't get a chance to read it. Leise's ringtone went off. *Speak of the devil.*

Ari grabbed her cell instead. "Leise? Finally, where are you?" The voice on the other end wasn't Leise, it wasn't female at all.

"No, Aramais. This is Brennan."

Ari's smile faltered somewhat, but she was still happy to hear from him. She turned away from Leif. "What's wrong?"

"You need to get here. I don't know how the legal system works in this time."

"Legal system? What happened?" Ari's mind raced with wild scenarios. Surely, this was just a misunderstanding.

"Annaleise is in jail… for murder."

The phone and the paper clutched in her hand, slipped from her fingers. Ari glanced down as Brennan's words sank in. In bold black letters, in her mother's handwriting were three simple words.

This is War.

The End

ACKNOWLEDGMENTS

I'd like to thank Nicole Flockton, my Tuesday writing partner, for always keeping me on the right path and inspiring me when the words refuse to come. Also teaching me about Sprints - Total Game Changer.

I am deeply grateful to Ken Wallen and Anesa Michalek for taking the time to help me work through my many story issues and even giving some Spanish tips along the way. You two are the best in so many ways. I am blessed to have you in my life.

And to my HMNS - Sugar Land VS crew: Arineh, Drayton, Tracy, Damian, Sarah, Cyan, Aaron, and Seth. You guys are awesome and you made everyday at work, not feel like work at all.

ABOUT THE AUTHOR

R.R. Born lives in Texas with her husband, and an orange tabby terror named Pele. She graduated from Houston Community College where she studied Photography, then graduated with a degree in Film from Long Island University in Brookville, NY. She's worked as a Production Coordinator, and Second Assistant Director on local commercials, TV shows, and movies.

For more info on upcoming books

http://www.rrborn.com

Thank you for reading
Day of the Dead

I hope you enjoyed Ari, Leif, and Jacque's story. In the next exciting installment of the Gray Witch series, **DEAD WRONG**, we will find out what happens to Ari, Leise, and Brennan in Ireland.

If you enjoyed this book, please take a few minutes and place a review on Amazon, Goodreads, or your favorite online retailer. It helps other readers who enjoy books about witches and magic find this one.
Leave a Review on Amazon - Just Click Here

SIGN UP FOR MY NEWSLETTER to find out when new books are released! www.rrborn.com/newsletter

Join my Facebook Page for exclusive giveaways, sneak peeks of future books.

Again, thank you.
R.R. Born

THE GRAY WITCH SERIES

Book 1 - May Day

Made in the USA
Columbia, SC
04 May 2022

59861071R00129